Disney · PIXAR

INCREDIBLES 2

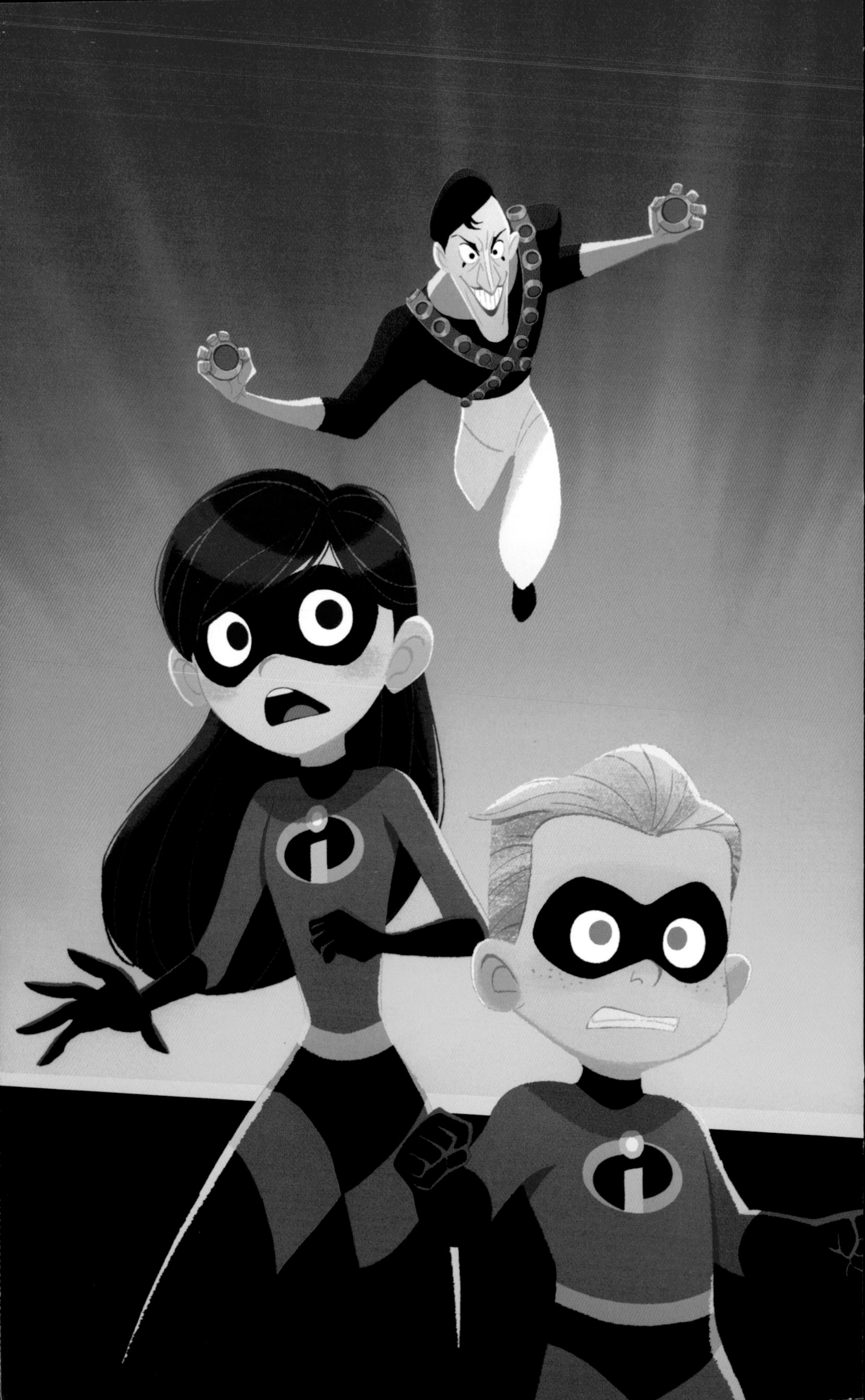

Disney · PIXAR
INCREDIBLES 2

CRISIS IN MID-LIFE!

Script **CHRISTOS GAGE**   Art **GURIHIRU**
Lettering **RICHARD STARKINGS** & **COMICRAFT'S JIMMY BETANCOURT**

BEDTIME STORY

Script **CHRISTOS GAGE**   Art **J BONE**   Colors **DAN JACKSON**
Lettering **RICHARD STARKINGS** & **COMICRAFT'S JIMMY BETANCOURT**

A RELAXING DAY AT THE PARK
and HOW THE COOKIE CRUMBLES

Scripts **LANDRY Q. WALKER**   Layouts **EMILIO URBANO**
Pencils **ANDREA GREPPI**   Inks **ROBERTA ZANOTTA**
Colors **ANGELA CAPOLUPO**   Lettering **CHRIS DICKEY**

Cover Art **GURIHIRU**

DARK HORSE BOOKS

DARK HORSE BOOKS

president and publisher
MIKE RICHARDSON

editor
FREDDYE MILLER

assistant editors
JUDY KHUU, JENNY BLENK, KEVIN BURKHALTER

designer
DAVID NESTELLE

digital art technician
CHRISTIANNE GILLENARDO-GOUDREAU

Neil Hankerson Executive Vice President • Tom Weddle Chief Financial Officer • Randy Stradley Vice President of Publishing • Nick McWhorter Chief Business Development Officer • Dale LaFountain Chief Information Officer • Matt Parkinson Vice President of Marketing • Cara Niece Vice President of Production and Scheduling • Mark Bernardi Vice President of Book Trade and Digital Sales • Ken Lizzi General Counsel • Dave Marshall Editor in Chief • Davey Estrada Editorial Director • Chris Warner Senior Books Editor • Cary Grazzini Director of Specialty Projects • Lia Ribacchi Art Director • Vanessa Todd-Holmes Director of Print Purchasing • Matt Dryer Director of Digital Art and Prepress • Michael Gombos Director of International Publishing and Licensing • Kari Yadro Director of Custom Programs • Kari Torson Director of International Licensing

DISNEY PUBLISHING WORLDWIDE GLOBAL MAGAZINES, COMICS AND PARTWORKS

PUBLISHER Lynn Waggoner • EDITORIAL TEAM Bianca Coletti (Director, Magazines), Guido Frazzini (Director, Comics), Carlotta Quattrocolo (Executive Editor), Stefano Ambrosio (Executive Editor, New IP), Camilla Vedove (Senior Manager, Editorial Development), Behnoosh Khalili (Senior Editor), Julie Dorris (Senior Editor), Mina Riazi (Assistant Editor), Jonathan Manning (Assistant Editor) • DESIGN Enrico Soave (Senior Designer) • ART Ken Shue (VP, Global Art), Manny Mederos (Senior Illustration Manager, Comics and Magazines), Roberto Santillo (Creative Director), Marco Ghiglione (Creative Manager), Stefano Attardi (Computer Art Designer) • PORTFOLIO MANAGEMENT • Olivia Ciancarelli (Director) • BUSINESS & MARKETING Mariantonietta Galla (Marketing Manager), Virpi Korhonen (Editorial Manager)

INCREDIBLES 2: CRISIS IN MID-LIFE! & OTHER STORIES

Published by Dark Horse Books
A division of Dark Horse Comics, Inc.
10956 SE Main Street
Milwaukie, OR 97222

DarkHorse.com

To find a comics shop in your area, visit comicshoplocator.com

First edition: February 2019
ISBN 978-1-50671-019-8

1 3 5 7 9 10 8 6 4 2
Printed in China

MEET THE PARR FAMILY—AKA . . .
THE INCREDIBLES!

BOB PARR "MR. INCREDIBLE"

Married to Elastigirl and father of three growing Supers, Bob has found that parenting is a truly heroic act. He has the power of mega-strength and invulnerability—and also an uncanny ability to sense danger.

HELEN PARR "ELASTIGIRL"

While she kept her hero identity dormant for years while taking on parenting, Helen was one of the best Supers in her heyday. She has the power to bend, stretch, and twist into any form.

VIOLET PARR

The oldest of the three Parr children. Fourteen years old, she is intelligent, sarcastic, and a little socially awkward—but she isn't afraid to speak her mind. Violet has the power to become invisible and create force fields.

DASHIELL "DASH" PARR

The middle child in the Parr family. Ten years old, he is adventurous, curious, competitive, and a little bit of a show-off. Dash has the power of super speed, and he doesn't want to hold back using it!

JACK-JACK PARR

In many ways he is a typical toddler—he talks baby-talk, makes messes at mealtime, and gets into things he shouldn't—but Jack-Jack is actually a polymorph and has an array of Super powers.

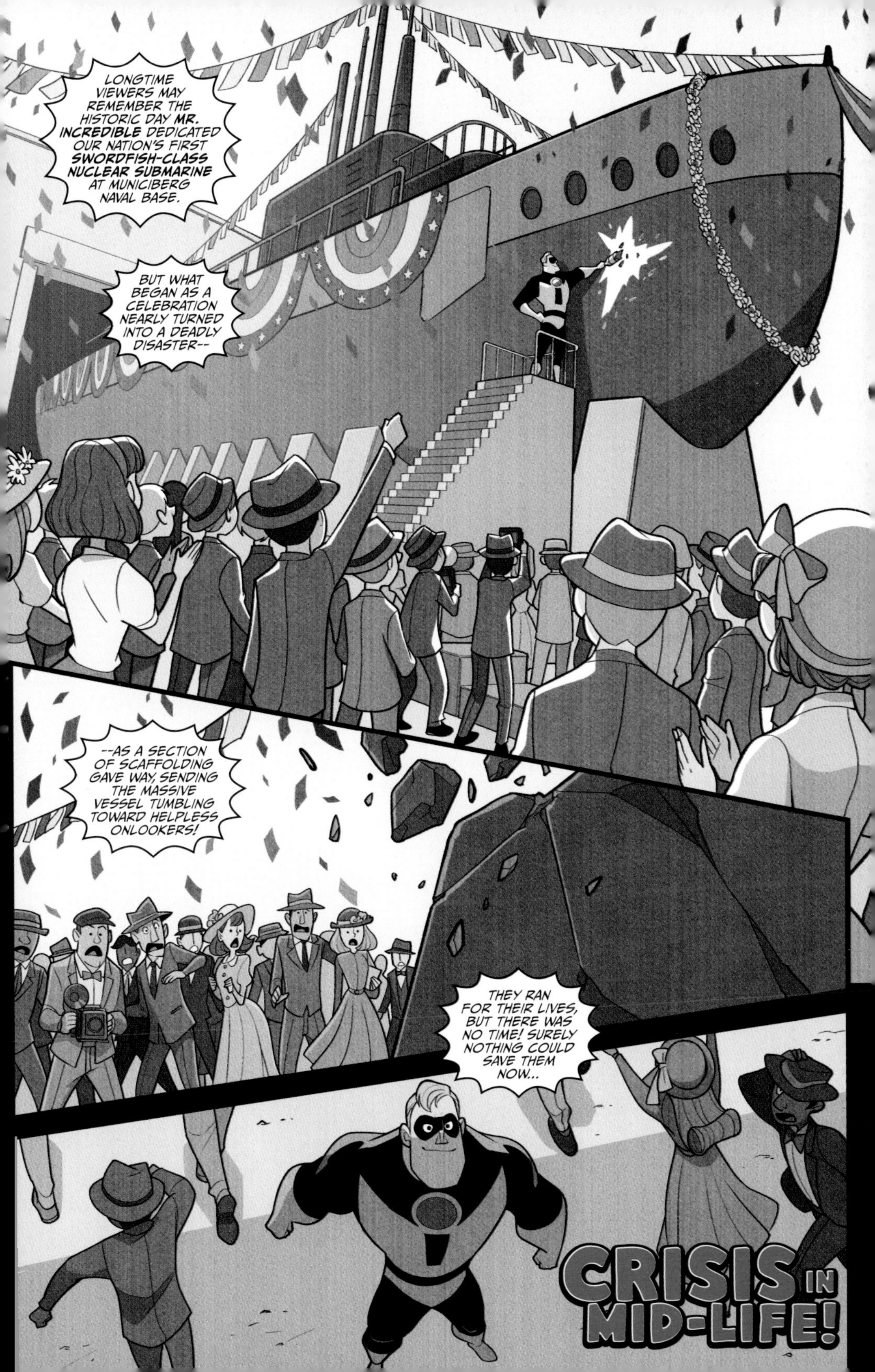
LONGTIME VIEWERS MAY REMEMBER THE HISTORIC DAY MR. INCREDIBLE DEDICATED OUR NATION'S FIRST SWORDFISH-CLASS NUCLEAR SUBMARINE AT MUNICIBERG NAVAL BASE.
BUT WHAT BEGAN AS A CELEBRATION NEARLY TURNED INTO A DEADLY DISASTER--
--AS A SECTION OF SCAFFOLDING GAVE WAY, SENDING THE MASSIVE VESSEL TUMBLING TOWARD HELPLESS ONLOOKERS!
THEY RAN FOR THEIR LIVES, BUT THERE WAS NO TIME! SURELY NOTHING COULD SAVE THEM NOW...
CRISIS IN MID-LIFE!

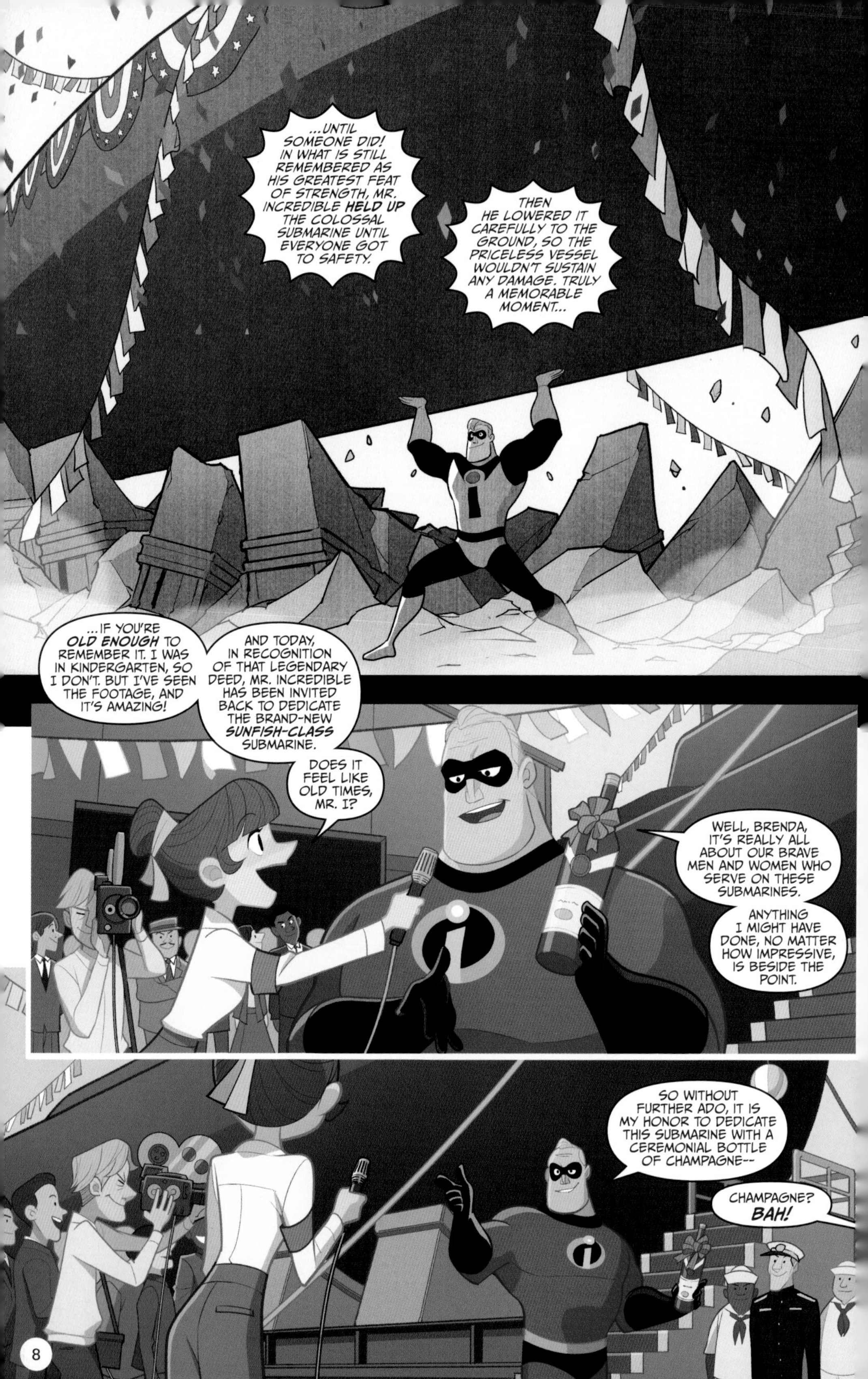
...UNTIL SOMEONE DID! IN WHAT IS STILL REMEMBERED AS HIS GREATEST FEAT OF STRENGTH, MR. INCREDIBLE HELD UP THE COLOSSAL SUBMARINE UNTIL EVERYONE GOT TO SAFETY.
THEN HE LOWERED IT CAREFULLY TO THE GROUND, SO THE PRICELESS VESSEL WOULDN'T SUSTAIN ANY DAMAGE. TRULY A MEMORABLE MOMENT...
...IF YOU'RE OLD ENOUGH TO REMEMBER IT. I WAS IN KINDERGARTEN, SO I DON'T. BUT I'VE SEEN THE FOOTAGE, AND IT'S AMAZING!
AND TODAY, IN RECOGNITION OF THAT LEGENDARY DEED, MR. INCREDIBLE HAS BEEN INVITED BACK TO DEDICATE THE BRAND-NEW SUNFISH-CLASS SUBMARINE.
DOES IT FEEL LIKE OLD TIMES, MR. I?
WELL, BRENDA, IT'S REALLY ALL ABOUT OUR BRAVE MEN AND WOMEN WHO SERVE ON THESE SUBMARINES.
ANYTHING I MIGHT HAVE DONE, NO MATTER HOW IMPRESSIVE, IS BESIDE THE POINT.
SO WITHOUT FURTHER ADO, IT IS MY HONOR TO DEDICATE THIS SUBMARINE WITH A CEREMONIAL BOTTLE OF CHAMPAGNE--
CHAMPAGNE? BAH!

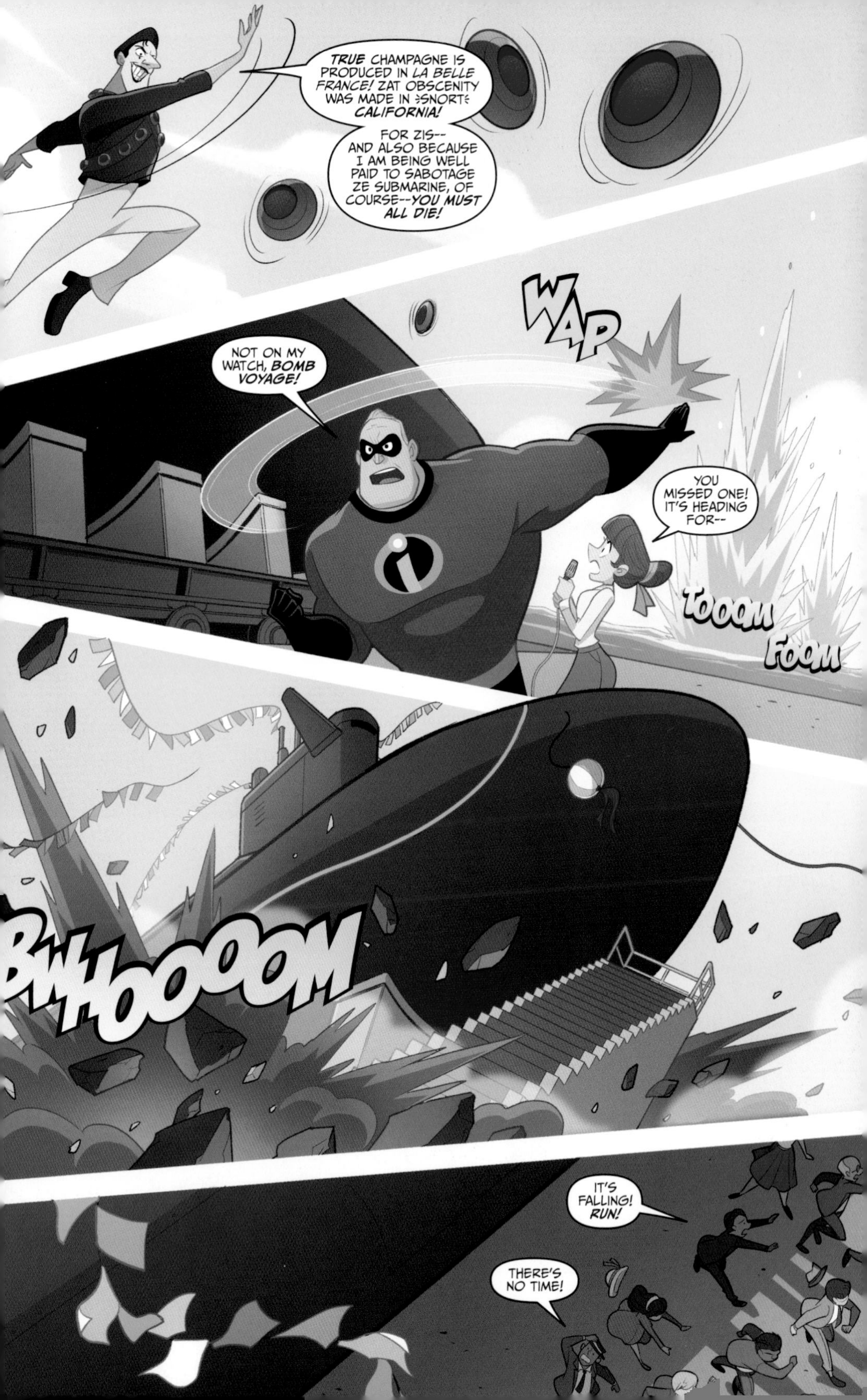
TRUE CHAMPAGNE IS PRODUCED IN LA BELLE FRANCE! ZAT OBSCENITY WAS MADE IN *SNORT* CALIFORNIA!
FOR ZIS-- AND ALSO BECAUSE I AM BEING WELL PAID TO SABOTAGE ZE SUBMARINE, OF COURSE--YOU MUST ALL DIE!
WAP
NOT ON MY WATCH, BOMB VOYAGE!
YOU MISSED ONE! IT'S HEADING FOR--
TOOOM
FOOM
BWHOOOOM
IT'S FALLING! RUN!
THERE'S NO TIME!

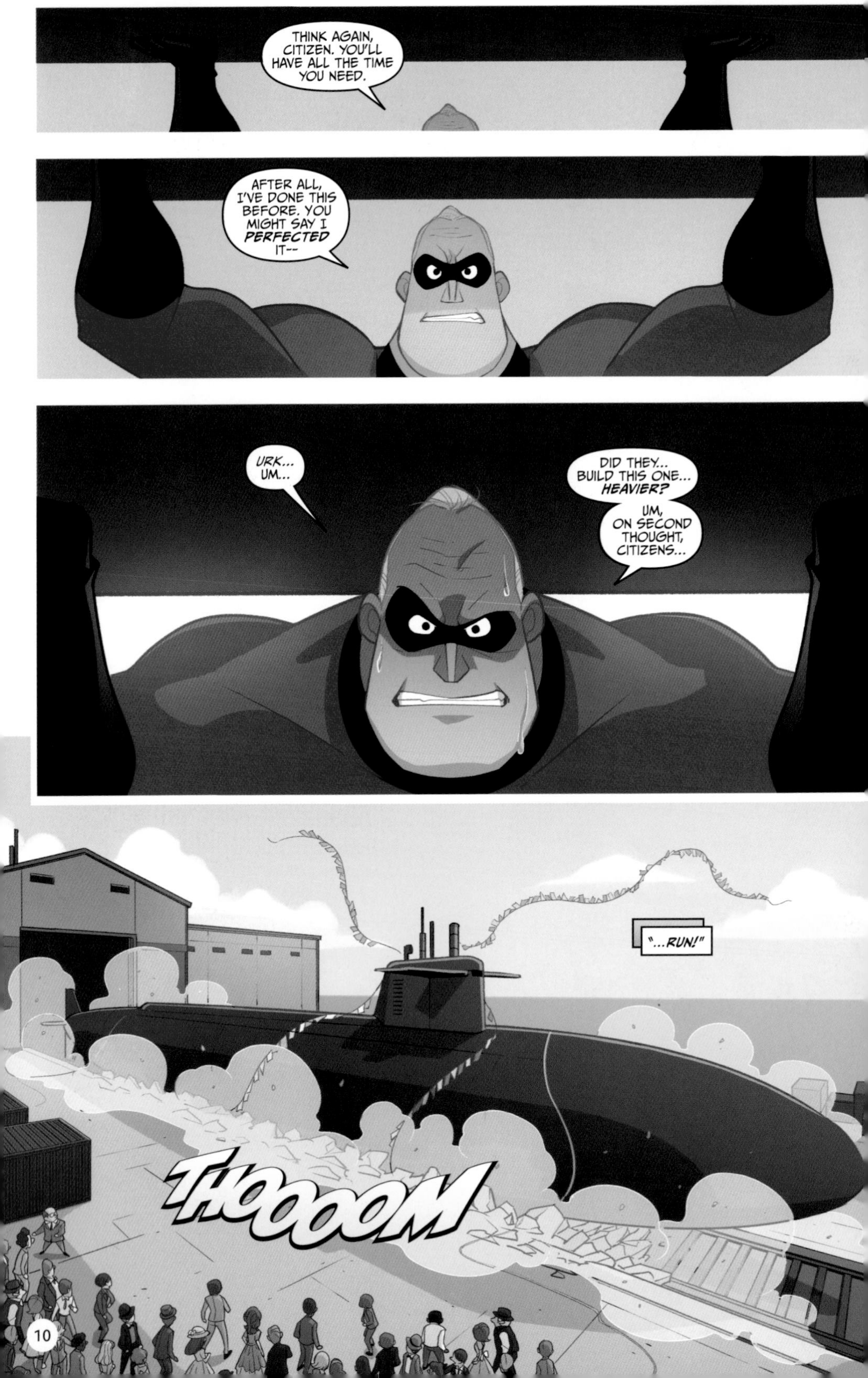
THINK AGAIN, CITIZEN. YOU'LL HAVE ALL THE TIME YOU NEED.
AFTER ALL, I'VE DONE THIS BEFORE. YOU MIGHT SAY I *PERFECTED* IT--
URK... UM...
DID THEY... BUILD THIS ONE... *HEAVIER?*
UM, ON SECOND THOUGHT, CITIZENS...
"...*RUN!*"
THOOOOM

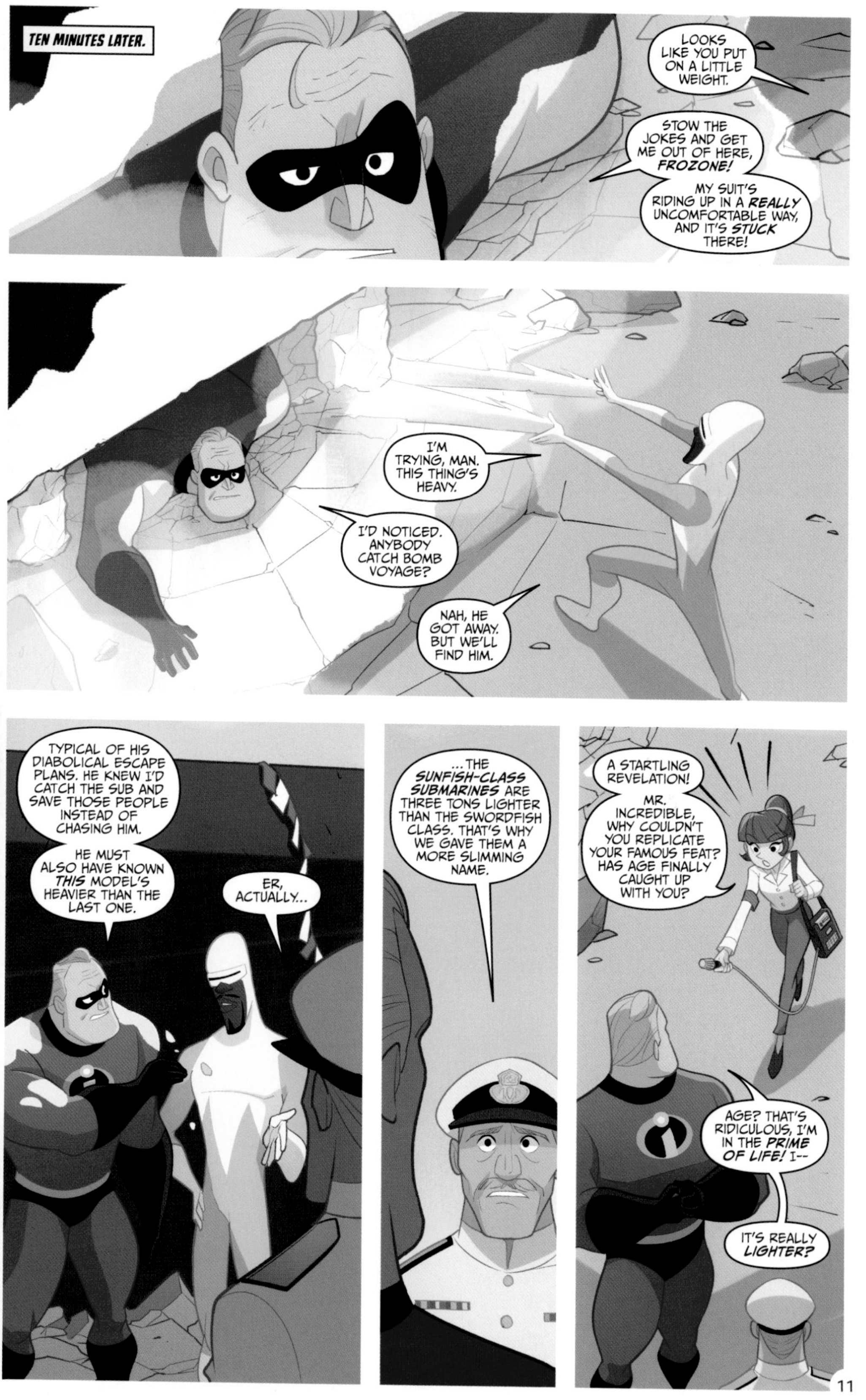
TEN MINUTES LATER.
LOOKS LIKE YOU PUT ON A LITTLE WEIGHT.
STOW THE JOKES AND GET ME OUT OF HERE, ***FROZONE!***
MY SUIT'S RIDING UP IN A ***REALLY*** UNCOMFORTABLE WAY, AND IT'S ***STUCK*** THERE!
I'M TRYING, MAN. THIS THING'S HEAVY.
I'D NOTICED. ANYBODY CATCH BOMB VOYAGE?
NAH, HE GOT AWAY. BUT WE'LL FIND HIM.
TYPICAL OF HIS DIABOLICAL ESCAPE PLANS. HE KNEW I'D CATCH THE SUB AND SAVE THOSE PEOPLE INSTEAD OF CHASING HIM.
HE MUST ALSO HAVE KNOWN ***THIS*** MODEL'S HEAVIER THAN THE LAST ONE.
ER, ACTUALLY...
...THE ***SUNFISH-CLASS SUBMARINES*** ARE THREE TONS LIGHTER THAN THE SWORDFISH CLASS. THAT'S WHY WE GAVE THEM A MORE SLIMMING NAME.
A STARTLING REVELATION!
MR. INCREDIBLE, WHY COULDN'T YOU REPLICATE YOUR FAMOUS FEAT? HAS AGE FINALLY CAUGHT UP WITH YOU?
AGE? THAT'S RIDICULOUS, I'M IN THE ***PRIME OF LIFE!*** I--
IT'S REALLY ***LIGHTER?***

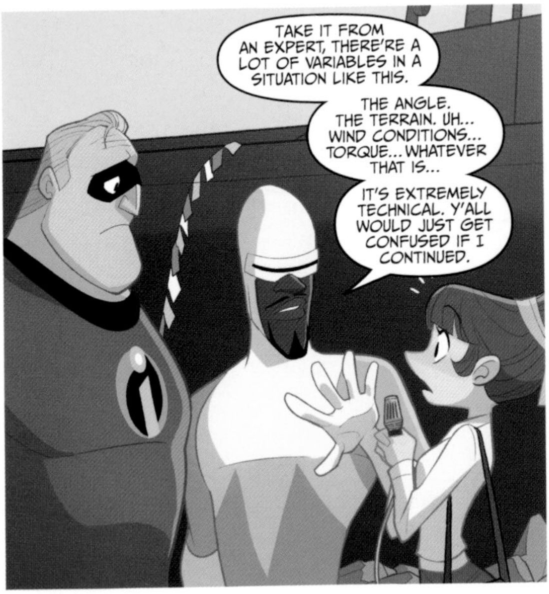
TAKE IT FROM AN EXPERT, THERE'RE A LOT OF VARIABLES IN A SITUATION LIKE THIS.
THE ANGLE. THE TERRAIN. UH... WIND CONDITIONS... TORQUE... WHATEVER THAT IS...
IT'S EXTREMELY TECHNICAL. Y'ALL WOULD JUST GET CONFUSED IF I CONTINUED.

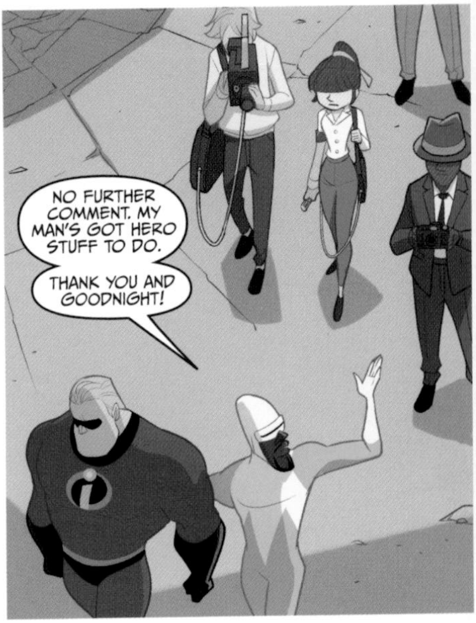
NO FURTHER COMMENT. MY MAN'S GOT HERO STUFF TO DO.
THANK YOU AND GOODNIGHT!

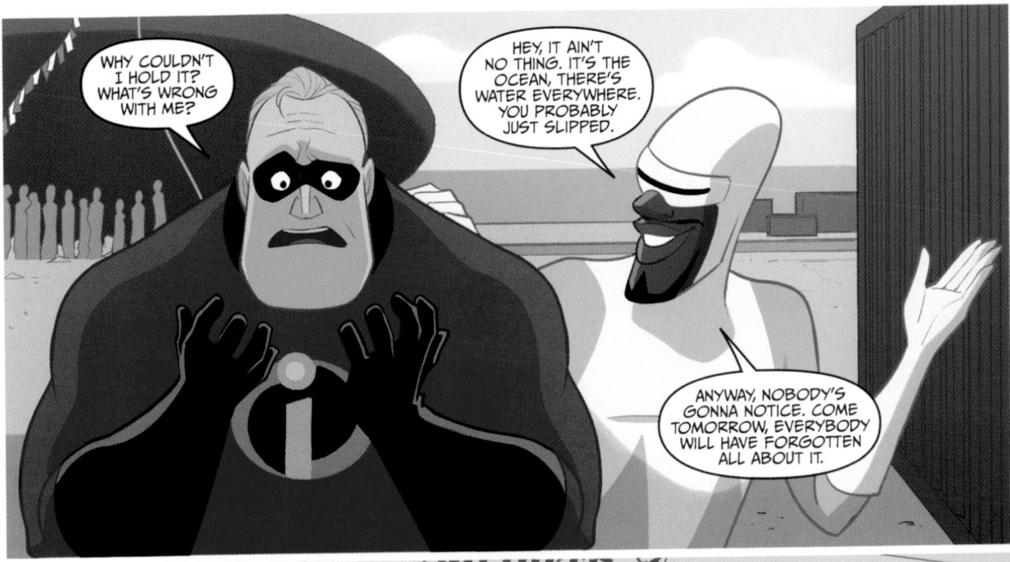
WHY COULDN'T I HOLD IT? WHAT'S WRONG WITH ME?
HEY, IT AIN'T NO THING. IT'S THE OCEAN, THERE'S WATER EVERYWHERE. YOU PROBABLY JUST SLIPPED.
ANYWAY, NOBODY'S GONNA NOTICE. COME TOMORROW, EVERYBODY WILL HAVE FORGOTTEN ALL ABOUT IT.

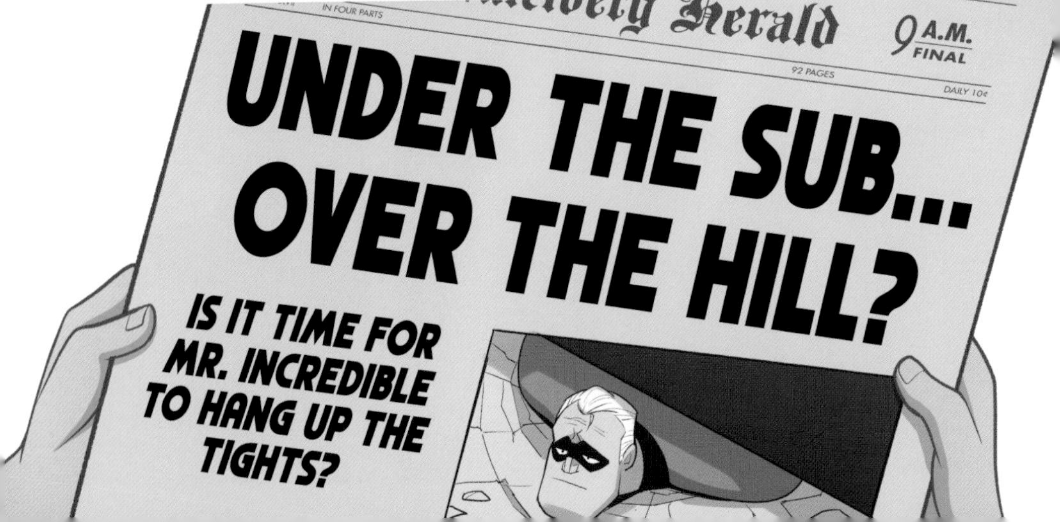
IN FOUR PARTS
9 A.M. FINAL
92 PAGES
DAILY 10¢
UNDER THE SUB... OVER THE HILL?
IS IT TIME FOR MR. INCREDIBLE TO HANG UP THE TIGHTS?

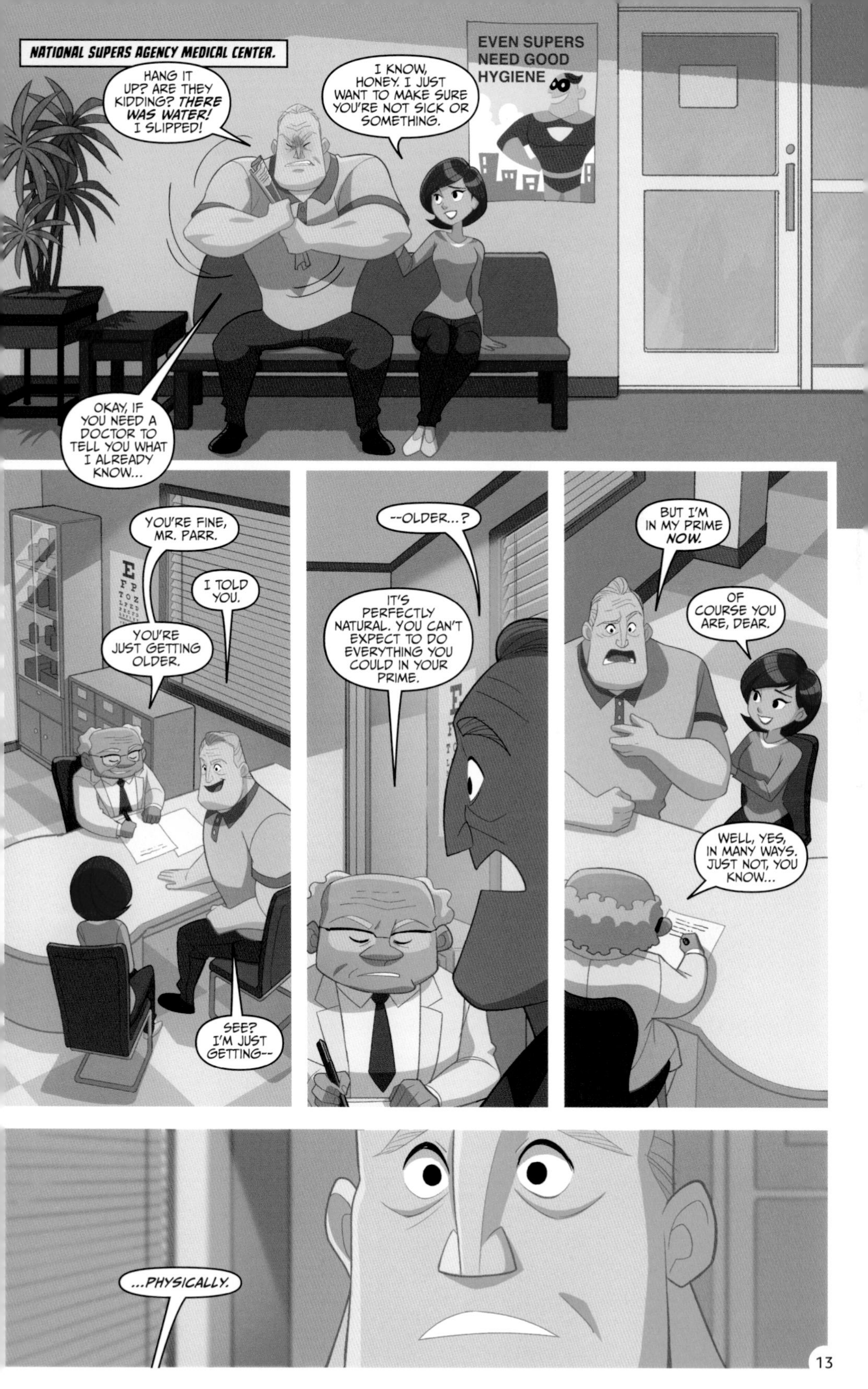
NATIONAL SUPERS AGENCY MEDICAL CENTER.
HANG IT UP? ARE THEY KIDDING? THERE WAS WATER! I SLIPPED!
I KNOW, HONEY. I JUST WANT TO MAKE SURE YOU'RE NOT SICK OR SOMETHING.
EVEN SUPERS NEED GOOD HYGIENE
OKAY, IF YOU NEED A DOCTOR TO TELL YOU WHAT I ALREADY KNOW...
YOU'RE FINE, MR. PARR.
I TOLD YOU.
YOU'RE JUST GETTING OLDER.
SEE? I'M JUST GETTING--
--OLDER...?
IT'S PERFECTLY NATURAL. YOU CAN'T EXPECT TO DO EVERYTHING YOU COULD IN YOUR PRIME.
BUT I'M IN MY PRIME NOW.
OF COURSE YOU ARE, DEAR.
WELL, YES, IN MANY WAYS. JUST NOT, YOU KNOW...
...PHYSICALLY.

THE PARR HOME.

IT'S ALL OVER, HELEN. I'M WASHED UP.

YOU'RE NOT WASHED UP, BOB.

DASH! NO SUPER SPEED AT THE TABLE!

THERE'S NOTHING SADDER THAN AN OLD HERO WHO DOESN'T KNOW WHEN TO QUIT.

YOU DON'T NEED TO QUIT.

VIOLET! BACKPACK!

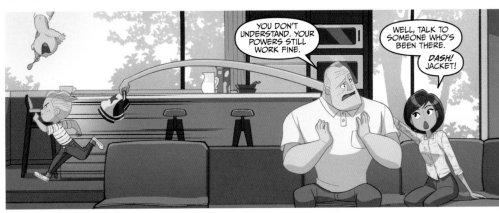

YOU DON'T UNDERSTAND. YOUR POWERS STILL WORK FINE.

WELL, TALK TO SOMEONE WHO'S BEEN THERE.

DASH! JACKET!

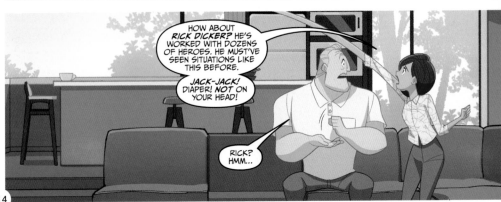

HOW ABOUT *RICK DICKER?* HE'S WORKED WITH DOZENS OF HEROES. HE MUST'VE SEEN SITUATIONS LIKE THIS BEFORE.

JACK-JACK! DIAPER! *NOT* ON YOUR HEAD!

RICK? HMM...

14

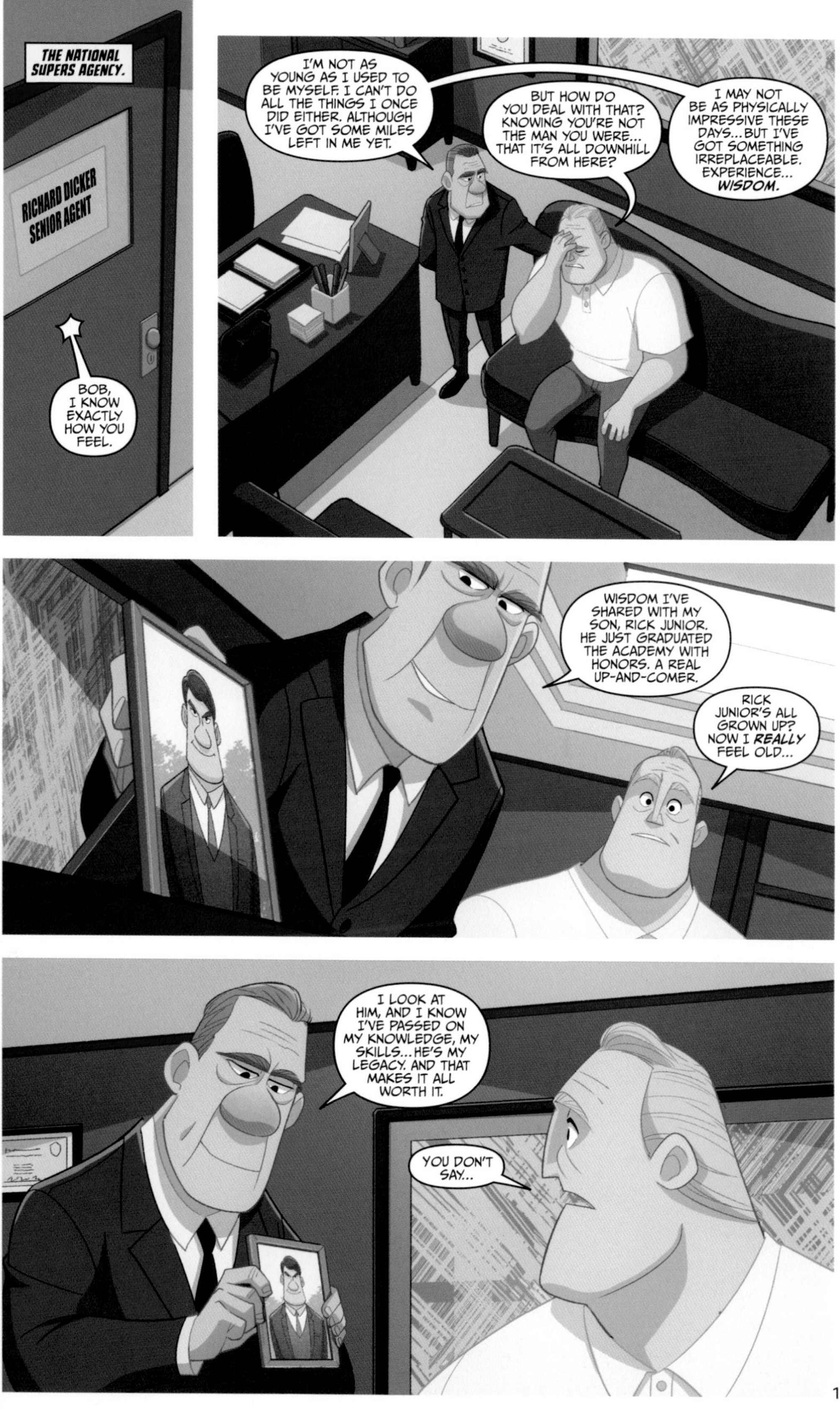
THE NATIONAL SUPERS AGENCY.
RICHARD DICKER SENIOR AGENT
BOB, I KNOW EXACTLY HOW YOU FEEL.
I'M NOT AS YOUNG AS I USED TO BE MYSELF. I CAN'T DO ALL THE THINGS I ONCE DID EITHER. ALTHOUGH I'VE GOT SOME MILES LEFT IN ME YET.
BUT HOW DO YOU DEAL WITH THAT? KNOWING YOU'RE NOT THE MAN YOU WERE... THAT IT'S ALL DOWNHILL FROM HERE?
I MAY NOT BE AS PHYSICALLY IMPRESSIVE THESE DAYS...BUT I'VE GOT SOMETHING IRREPLACEABLE. EXPERIENCE... WISDOM.
WISDOM I'VE SHARED WITH MY SON, RICK JUNIOR. HE JUST GRADUATED THE ACADEMY WITH HONORS. A REAL UP-AND-COMER.
RICK JUNIOR'S ALL GROWN UP? NOW I REALLY FEEL OLD...
I LOOK AT HIM, AND I KNOW I'VE PASSED ON MY KNOWLEDGE, MY SKILLS...HE'S MY LEGACY. AND THAT MAKES IT ALL WORTH IT.
YOU DON'T SAY...

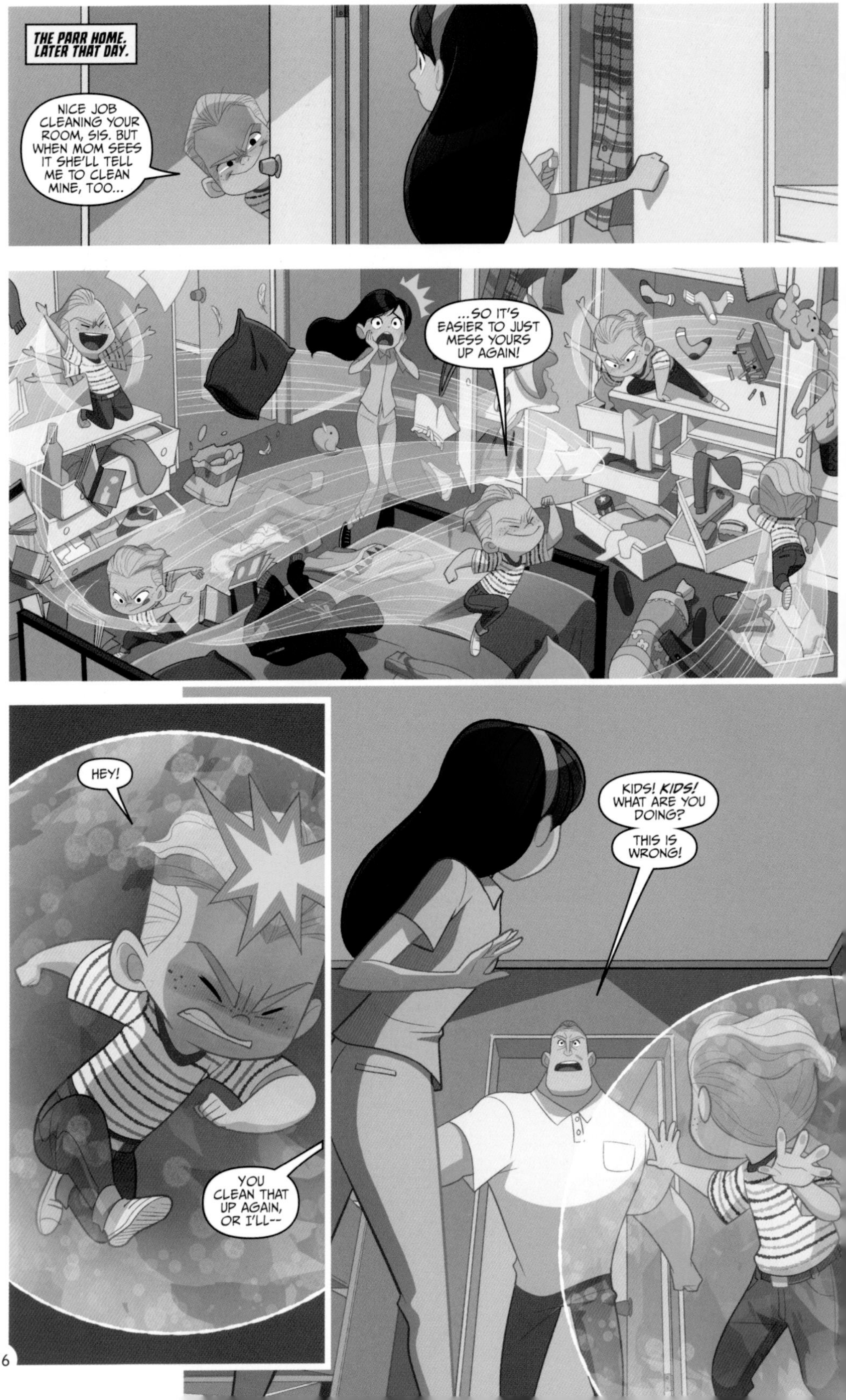
THE PARR HOME. LATER THAT DAY.
NICE JOB CLEANING YOUR ROOM, SIS. BUT WHEN MOM SEES IT SHE'LL TELL ME TO CLEAN MINE, TOO...
...SO IT'S EASIER TO JUST MESS YOURS UP AGAIN!
HEY!
YOU CLEAN THAT UP AGAIN, OR I'LL--
KIDS! *KIDS!* WHAT ARE YOU DOING?
THIS IS WRONG!

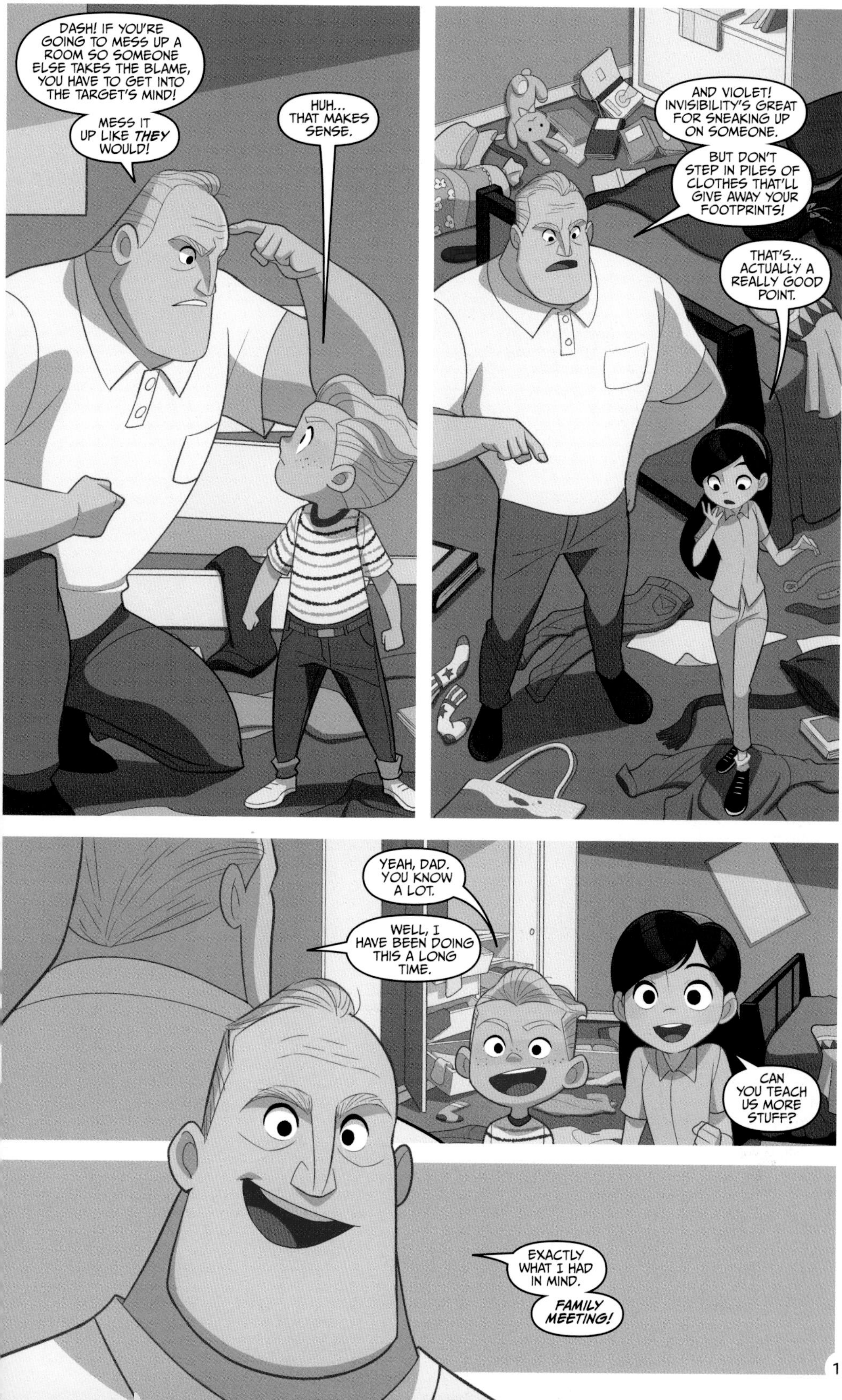
DASH! IF YOU'RE GOING TO MESS UP A ROOM SO SOMEONE ELSE TAKES THE BLAME, YOU HAVE TO GET INTO THE TARGET'S MIND!
MESS IT UP LIKE *THEY* WOULD!
HUH... THAT MAKES SENSE.
AND VIOLET! INVISIBILITY'S GREAT FOR SNEAKING UP ON SOMEONE.
BUT DON'T STEP IN PILES OF CLOTHES THAT'LL GIVE AWAY YOUR FOOTPRINTS!
THAT'S... ACTUALLY A REALLY GOOD POINT.
YEAH, DAD. YOU KNOW A LOT.
WELL, I HAVE BEEN DOING THIS A LONG TIME.
CAN YOU TEACH US MORE STUFF?
EXACTLY WHAT I HAD IN MIND.
FAMILY MEETING!

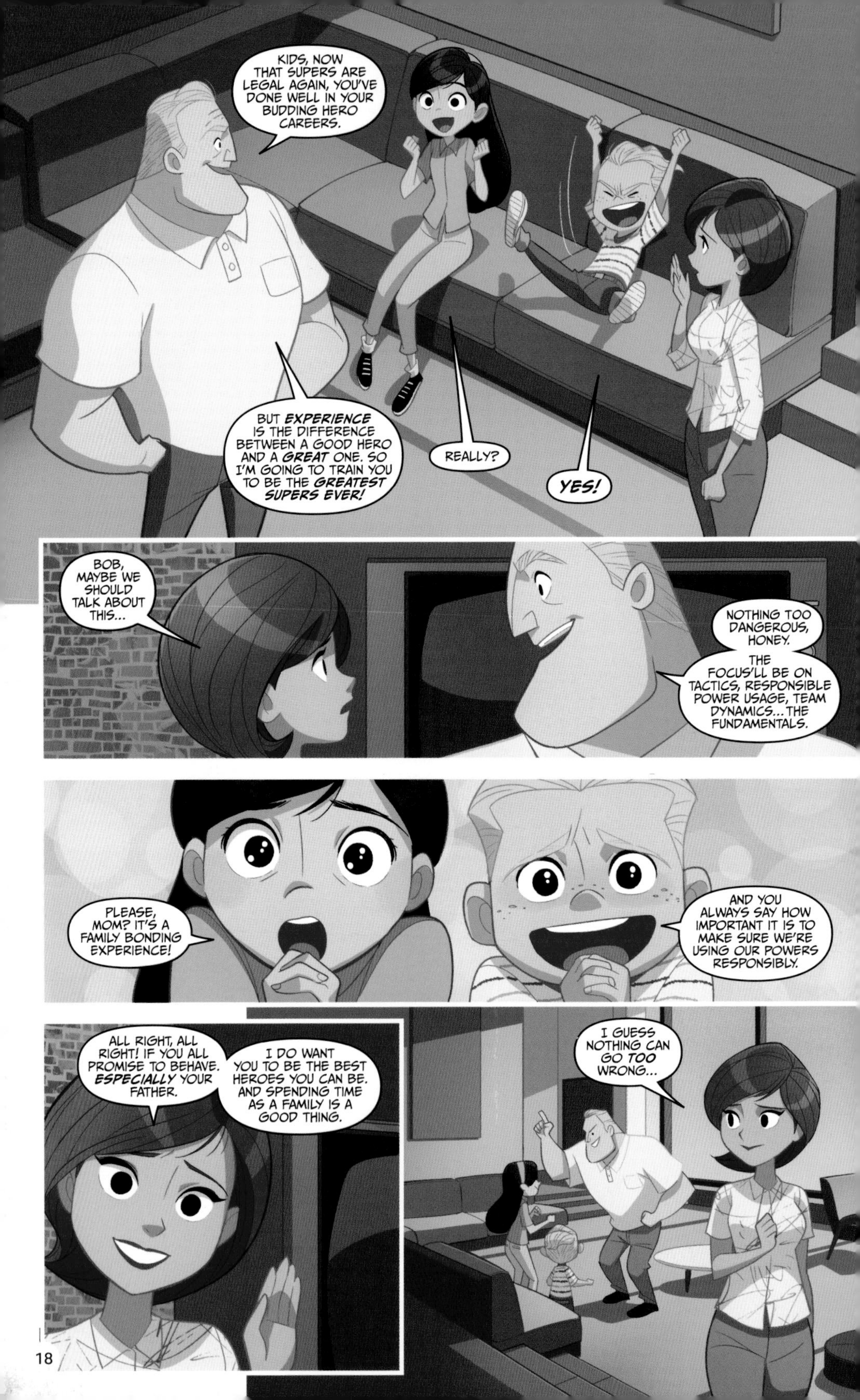
KIDS, NOW THAT SUPERS ARE LEGAL AGAIN, YOU'VE DONE WELL IN YOUR BUDDING HERO CAREERS.
BUT *EXPERIENCE* IS THE DIFFERENCE BETWEEN A GOOD HERO AND A *GREAT* ONE. SO I'M GOING TO TRAIN YOU TO BE THE *GREATEST SUPERS EVER!*
REALLY?
YES!
BOB, MAYBE WE SHOULD TALK ABOUT THIS...
NOTHING TOO DANGEROUS, HONEY.
THE FOCUS'LL BE ON TACTICS, RESPONSIBLE POWER USAGE, TEAM DYNAMICS... THE FUNDAMENTALS.
PLEASE, MOM? IT'S A FAMILY BONDING EXPERIENCE!
AND YOU ALWAYS SAY HOW IMPORTANT IT IS TO MAKE SURE WE'RE USING OUR POWERS RESPONSIBLY.
ALL RIGHT, ALL RIGHT! IF YOU ALL PROMISE TO BEHAVE. *ESPECIALLY* YOUR FATHER.
I DO WANT YOU TO BE THE BEST HEROES YOU CAN BE. AND SPENDING TIME AS A FAMILY IS A GOOD THING.
I GUESS NOTHING CAN GO *TOO* WRONG...

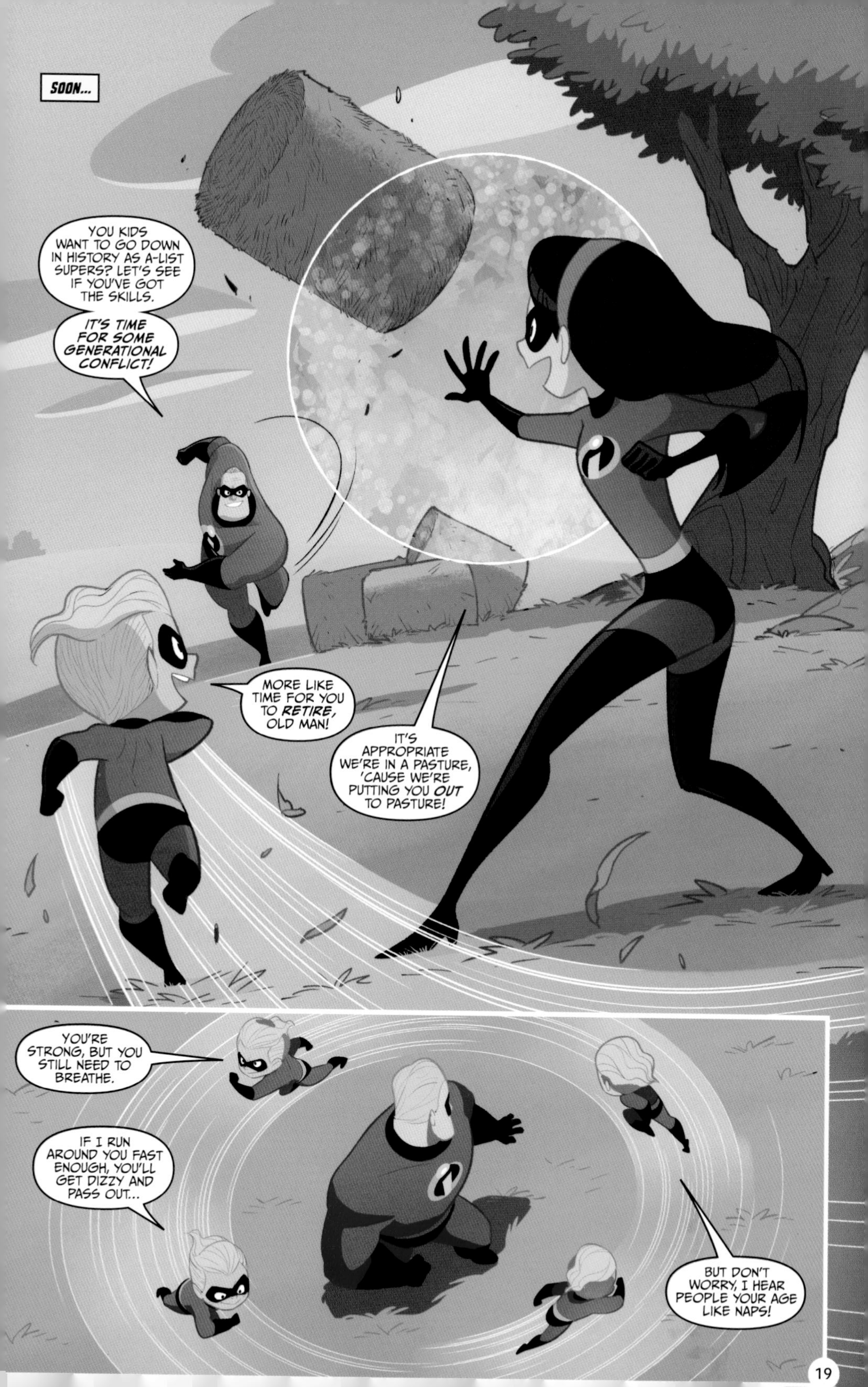
SOON...
YOU KIDS WANT TO GO DOWN IN HISTORY AS A-LIST SUPERS? LET'S SEE IF YOU'VE GOT THE SKILLS.
IT'S TIME FOR SOME GENERATIONAL CONFLICT!
MORE LIKE TIME FOR YOU TO RETIRE, OLD MAN!
IT'S APPROPRIATE WE'RE IN A PASTURE, 'CAUSE WE'RE PUTTING YOU OUT TO PASTURE!
YOU'RE STRONG, BUT YOU STILL NEED TO BREATHE.
IF I RUN AROUND YOU FAST ENOUGH, YOU'LL GET DIZZY AND PASS OUT...
BUT DON'T WORRY, I HEAR PEOPLE YOUR AGE LIKE NAPS!

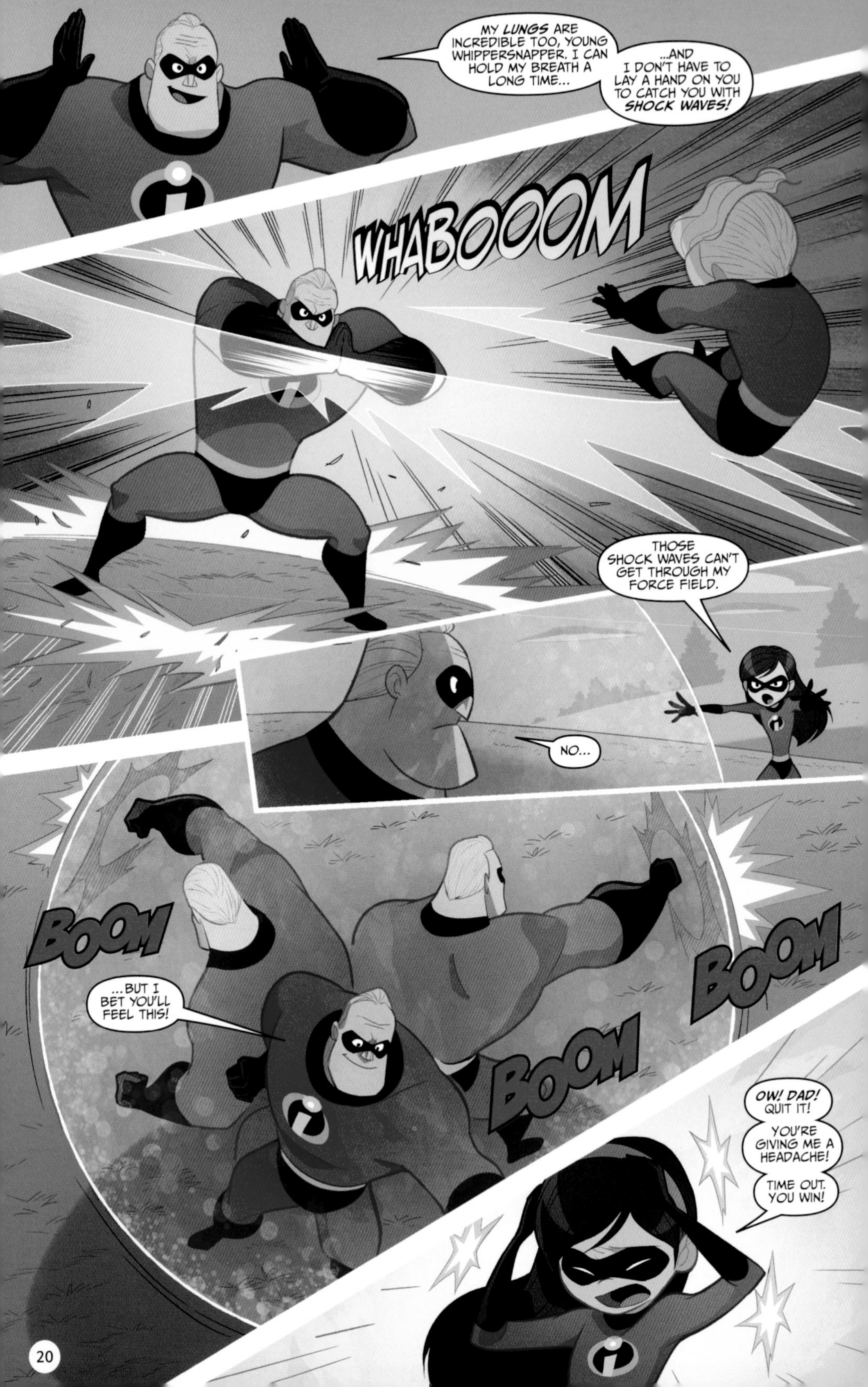
MY LUNGS ARE INCREDIBLE TOO, YOUNG WHIPPERSNAPPER. I CAN HOLD MY BREATH A LONG TIME...
...AND I DON'T HAVE TO LAY A HAND ON YOU TO CATCH YOU WITH SHOCK WAVES!
WHABOOOM
THOSE SHOCK WAVES CAN'T GET THROUGH MY FORCE FIELD.
NO...
BOOM
...BUT I BET YOU'LL FEEL THIS!
BOOM
BOOM
OW! DAD! QUIT IT!
YOU'RE GIVING ME A HEADACHE!
TIME OUT. YOU WIN!

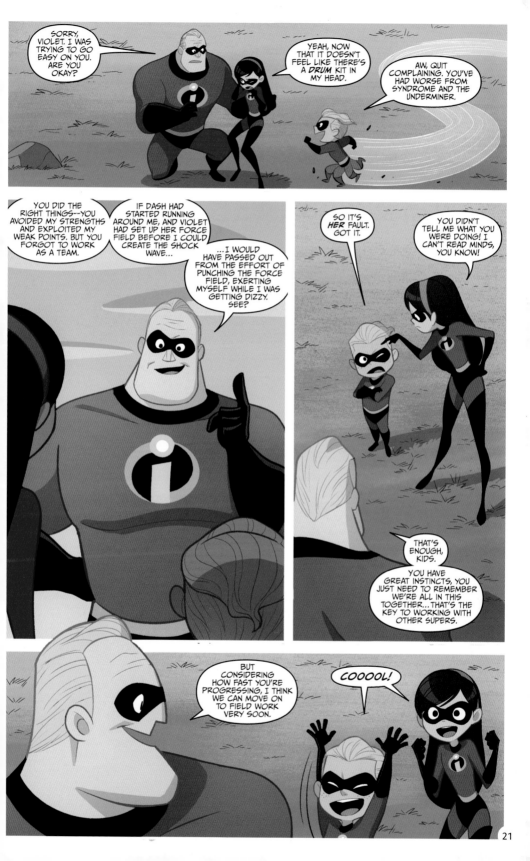

SORRY, VIOLET. I WAS TRYING TO GO EASY ON YOU. ARE YOU OKAY?

YEAH, NOW THAT IT DOESN'T FEEL LIKE THERE'S A *DRUM* KIT IN MY HEAD.

AW, QUIT COMPLAINING. YOU'VE HAD WORSE FROM SYNDROME AND THE UNDERMINER.

YOU DID THE RIGHT THINGS--YOU AVOIDED MY STRENGTHS AND EXPLOITED MY WEAK POINTS. BUT YOU FORGOT TO WORK AS A TEAM.

IF DASH HAD STARTED RUNNING AROUND ME, AND VIOLET HAD SET UP HER FORCE FIELD BEFORE I COULD CREATE THE SHOCK WAVE...

...I WOULD HAVE PASSED OUT FROM THE EFFORT OF PUNCHING THE FORCE FIELD, EXERTING MYSELF WHILE I WAS GETTING DIZZY. SEE?

SO IT'S *HER* FAULT. GOT IT.

YOU DIDN'T TELL ME WHAT YOU WERE DOING! I CAN'T READ MINDS, YOU KNOW!

THAT'S ENOUGH, KIDS.

YOU HAVE GREAT INSTINCTS, YOU JUST NEED TO REMEMBER WE'RE ALL IN THIS TOGETHER... THAT'S THE KEY TO WORKING WITH OTHER SUPERS.

BUT CONSIDERING HOW FAST YOU'RE PROGRESSING, I THINK WE CAN MOVE ON TO FIELD WORK VERY SOON.

COOOOL!

21

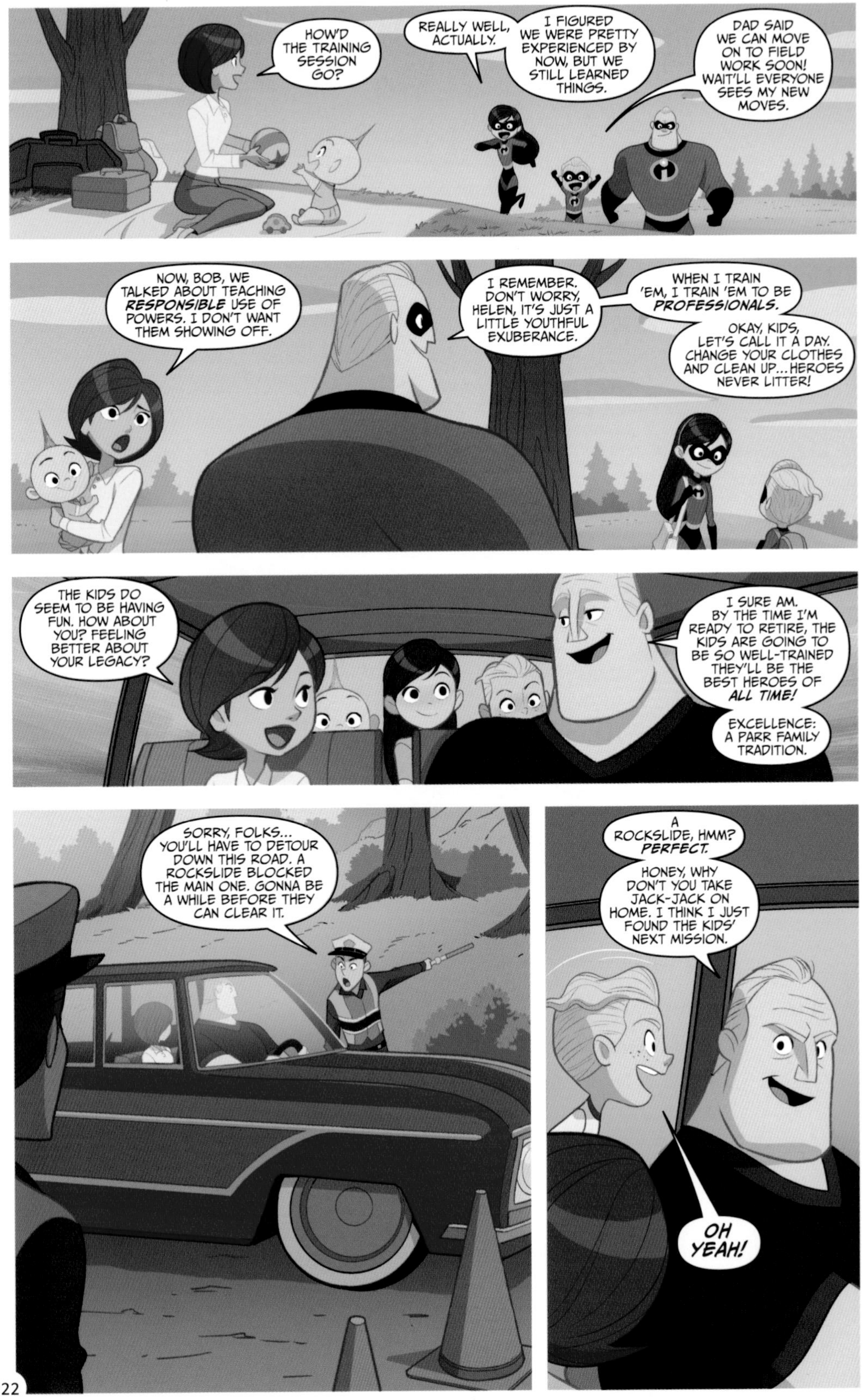

HOW'D THE TRAINING SESSION GO?
REALLY WELL, ACTUALLY.
I FIGURED WE WERE PRETTY EXPERIENCED BY NOW, BUT WE STILL LEARNED THINGS.
DAD SAID WE CAN MOVE ON TO FIELD WORK SOON! WAIT'LL EVERYONE SEES MY NEW MOVES.
NOW, BOB, WE TALKED ABOUT TEACHING RESPONSIBLE USE OF POWERS. I DON'T WANT THEM SHOWING OFF.
I REMEMBER. DON'T WORRY, HELEN, IT'S JUST A LITTLE YOUTHFUL EXUBERANCE.
WHEN I TRAIN 'EM, I TRAIN 'EM TO BE PROFESSIONALS.
OKAY, KIDS, LET'S CALL IT A DAY. CHANGE YOUR CLOTHES AND CLEAN UP... HEROES NEVER LITTER!
THE KIDS DO SEEM TO BE HAVING FUN. HOW ABOUT YOU? FEELING BETTER ABOUT YOUR LEGACY?
I SURE AM. BY THE TIME I'M READY TO RETIRE, THE KIDS ARE GOING TO BE SO WELL-TRAINED THEY'LL BE THE BEST HEROES OF ALL TIME!
EXCELLENCE: A PARR FAMILY TRADITION.
SORRY, FOLKS... YOU'LL HAVE TO DETOUR DOWN THIS ROAD. A ROCKSLIDE BLOCKED THE MAIN ONE. GONNA BE A WHILE BEFORE THEY CAN CLEAR IT.
A ROCKSLIDE, HMM? PERFECT.
HONEY, WHY DON'T YOU TAKE JACK-JACK ON HOME. I THINK I JUST FOUND THE KIDS' NEXT MISSION.
OH YEAH!

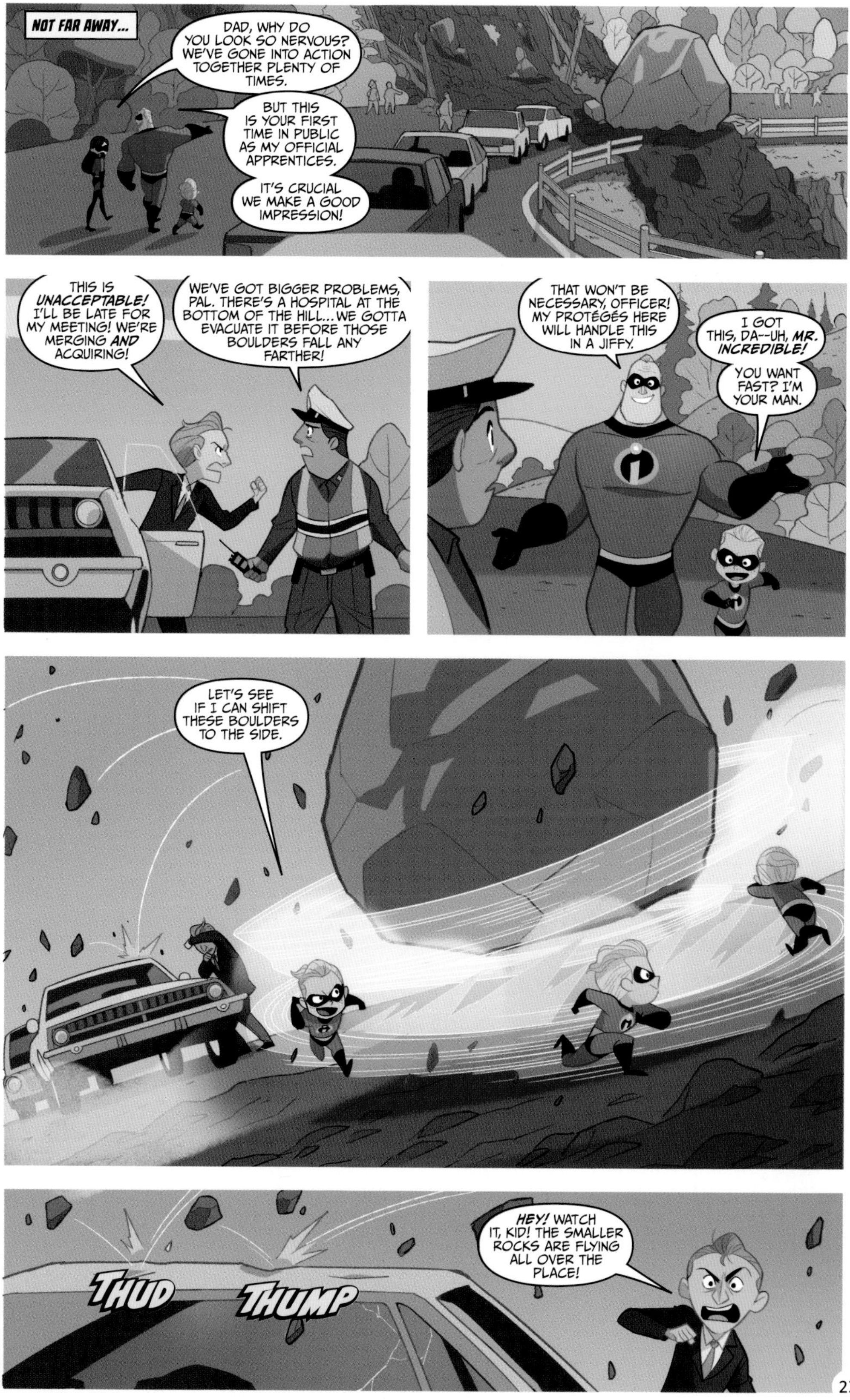
NOT FAR AWAY...
DAD, WHY DO YOU LOOK SO NERVOUS? WE'VE GONE INTO ACTION TOGETHER PLENTY OF TIMES.
BUT THIS IS YOUR FIRST TIME IN PUBLIC AS MY OFFICIAL APPRENTICES.
IT'S CRUCIAL WE MAKE A GOOD IMPRESSION!
THIS IS *UNACCEPTABLE!* I'LL BE LATE FOR MY MEETING! WE'RE MERGING *AND* ACQUIRING!
WE'VE GOT BIGGER PROBLEMS, PAL. THERE'S A HOSPITAL AT THE BOTTOM OF THE HILL... WE GOTTA EVACUATE IT BEFORE THOSE BOULDERS FALL ANY FARTHER!
THAT WON'T BE NECESSARY, OFFICER! MY PROTÉGÉS HERE WILL HANDLE THIS IN A JIFFY.
I GOT THIS, DA--UH, ***MR. INCREDIBLE!***
YOU WANT FAST? I'M YOUR MAN.
LET'S SEE IF I CAN SHIFT THESE BOULDERS TO THE SIDE.
THUD
THUMP
HEY! WATCH IT, KID! THE SMALLER ROCKS ARE FLYING ALL OVER THE PLACE!

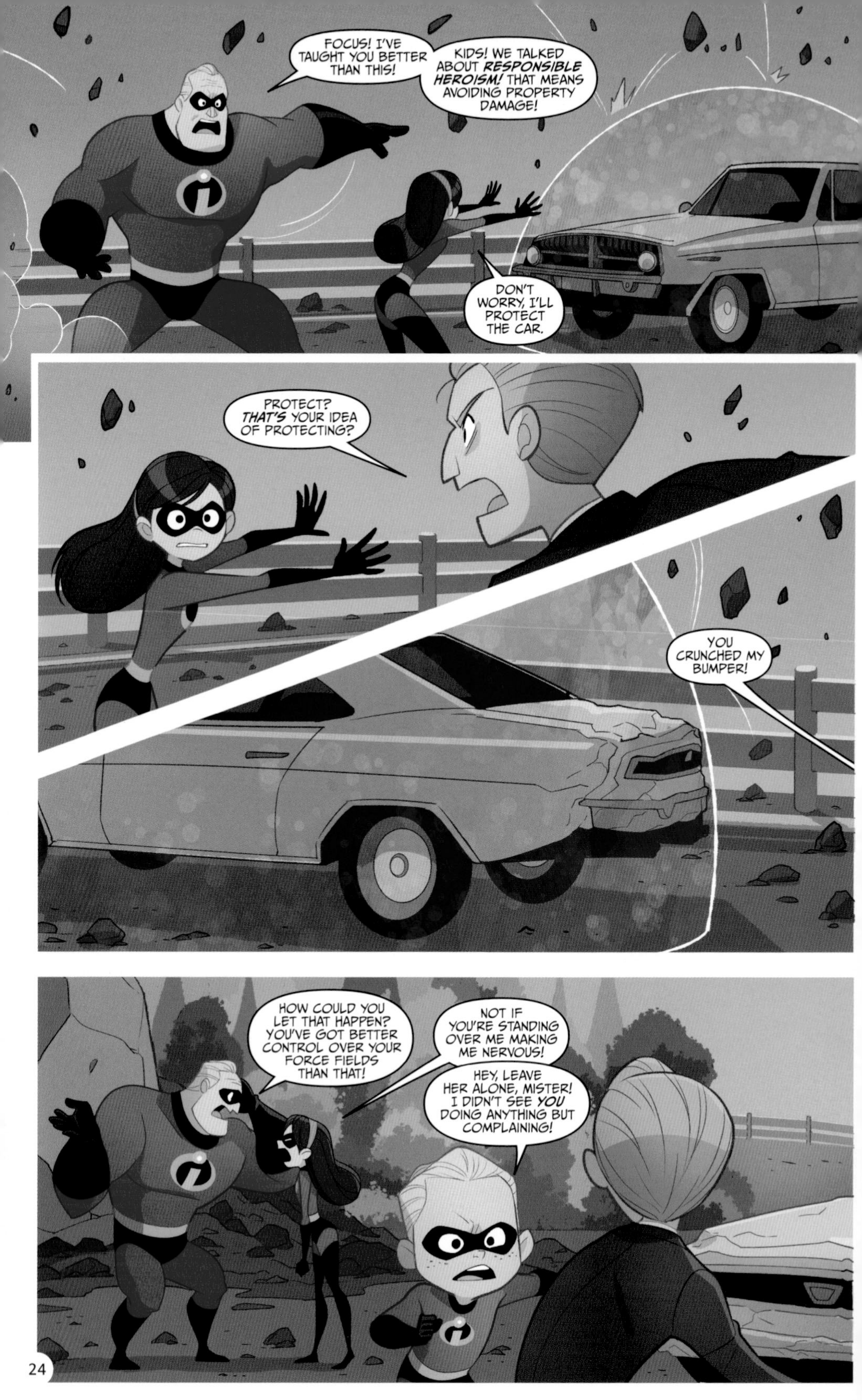
FOCUS! I'VE TAUGHT YOU BETTER THAN THIS!
KIDS! WE TALKED ABOUT RESPONSIBLE HEROISM! THAT MEANS AVOIDING PROPERTY DAMAGE!
DON'T WORRY, I'LL PROTECT THE CAR.
PROTECT? THAT'S YOUR IDEA OF PROTECTING?
YOU CRUNCHED MY BUMPER!
HOW COULD YOU LET THAT HAPPEN? YOU'VE GOT BETTER CONTROL OVER YOUR FORCE FIELDS THAN THAT!
NOT IF YOU'RE STANDING OVER ME MAKING ME NERVOUS!
HEY, LEAVE HER ALONE, MISTER! I DIDN'T SEE YOU DOING ANYTHING BUT COMPLAINING!

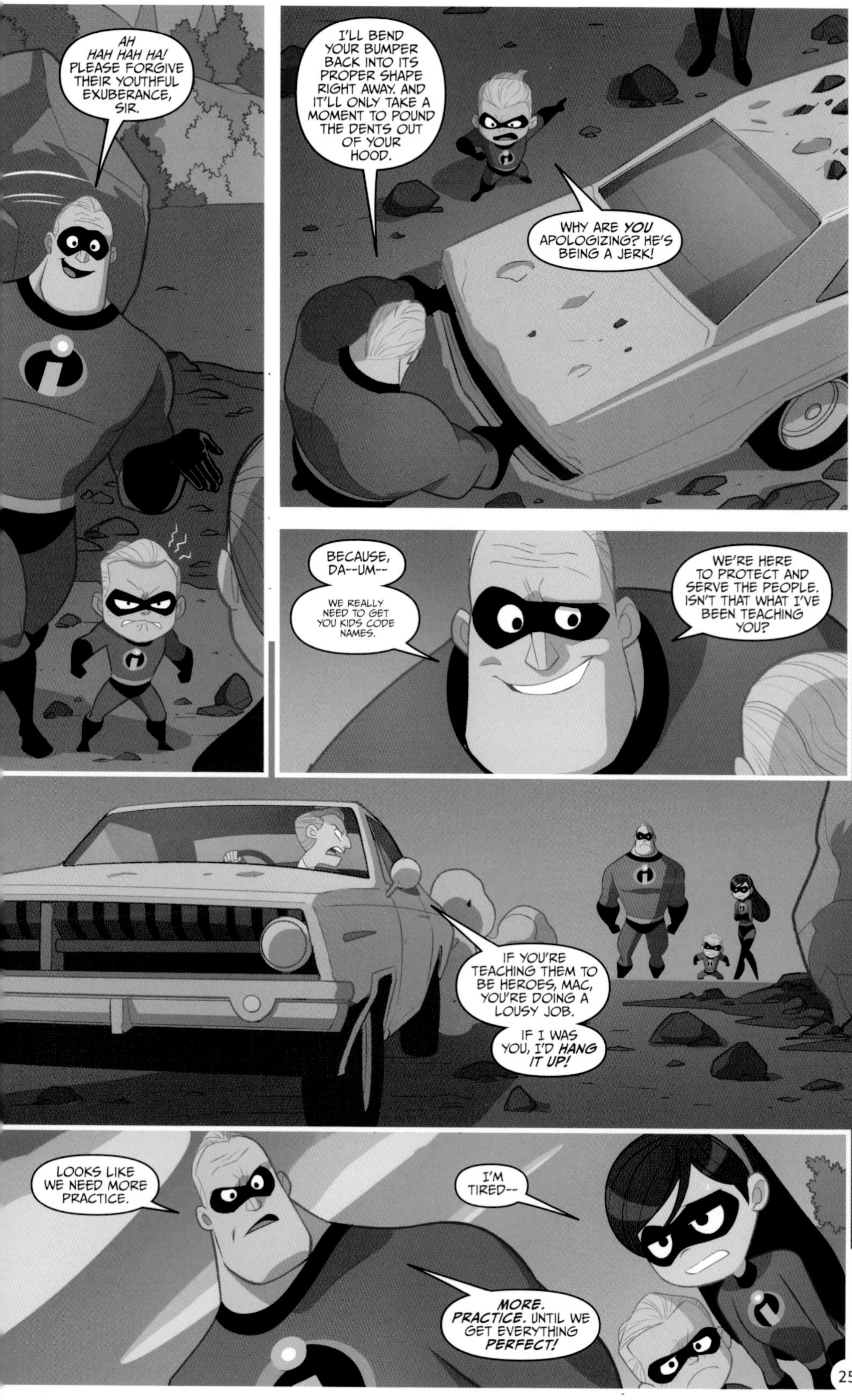
AH HAH HAH HA! PLEASE FORGIVE THEIR YOUTHFUL EXUBERANCE, SIR.
I'LL BEND YOUR BUMPER BACK INTO ITS PROPER SHAPE RIGHT AWAY. AND IT'LL ONLY TAKE A MOMENT TO POUND THE DENTS OUT OF YOUR HOOD.
WHY ARE YOU APOLOGIZING? HE'S BEING A JERK!
BECAUSE, DA--UM--
WE REALLY NEED TO GET YOU KIDS CODE NAMES.
WE'RE HERE TO PROTECT AND SERVE THE PEOPLE. ISN'T THAT WHAT I'VE BEEN TEACHING YOU?
IF YOU'RE TEACHING THEM TO BE HEROES, MAC, YOU'RE DOING A LOUSY JOB.
IF I WAS YOU, I'D HANG IT UP!
LOOKS LIKE WE NEED MORE PRACTICE.
I'M TIRED--
MORE. PRACTICE. UNTIL WE GET EVERYTHING PERFECT!

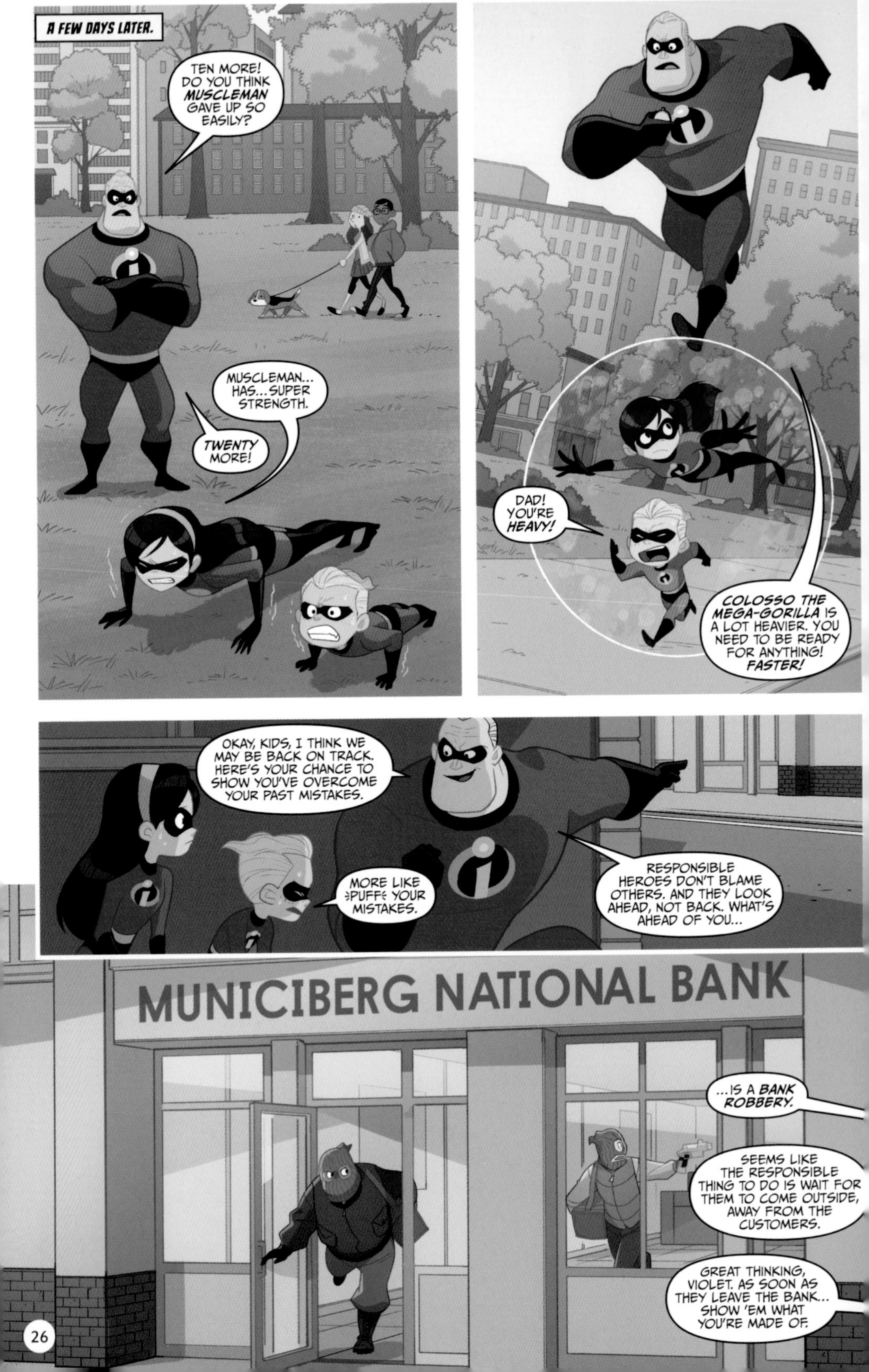
A FEW DAYS LATER.
TEN MORE! DO YOU THINK MUSCLEMAN GAVE UP SO EASILY?
MUSCLEMAN... HAS... SUPER STRENGTH.
TWENTY MORE!
DAD! YOU'RE HEAVY!
COLOSSO THE MEGA-GORILLA IS A LOT HEAVIER. YOU NEED TO BE READY FOR ANYTHING! FASTER!
OKAY, KIDS, I THINK WE MAY BE BACK ON TRACK. HERE'S YOUR CHANCE TO SHOW YOU'VE OVERCOME YOUR PAST MISTAKES.
MORE LIKE ⋟PUFF⋞ YOUR MISTAKES.
RESPONSIBLE HEROES DON'T BLAME OTHERS. AND THEY LOOK AHEAD, NOT BACK. WHAT'S AHEAD OF YOU...
MUNICIBERG NATIONAL BANK
...IS A BANK ROBBERY.
SEEMS LIKE THE RESPONSIBLE THING TO DO IS WAIT FOR THEM TO COME OUTSIDE, AWAY FROM THE CUSTOMERS.
GREAT THINKING, VIOLET. AS SOON AS THEY LEAVE THE BANK... SHOW 'EM WHAT YOU'RE MADE OF.

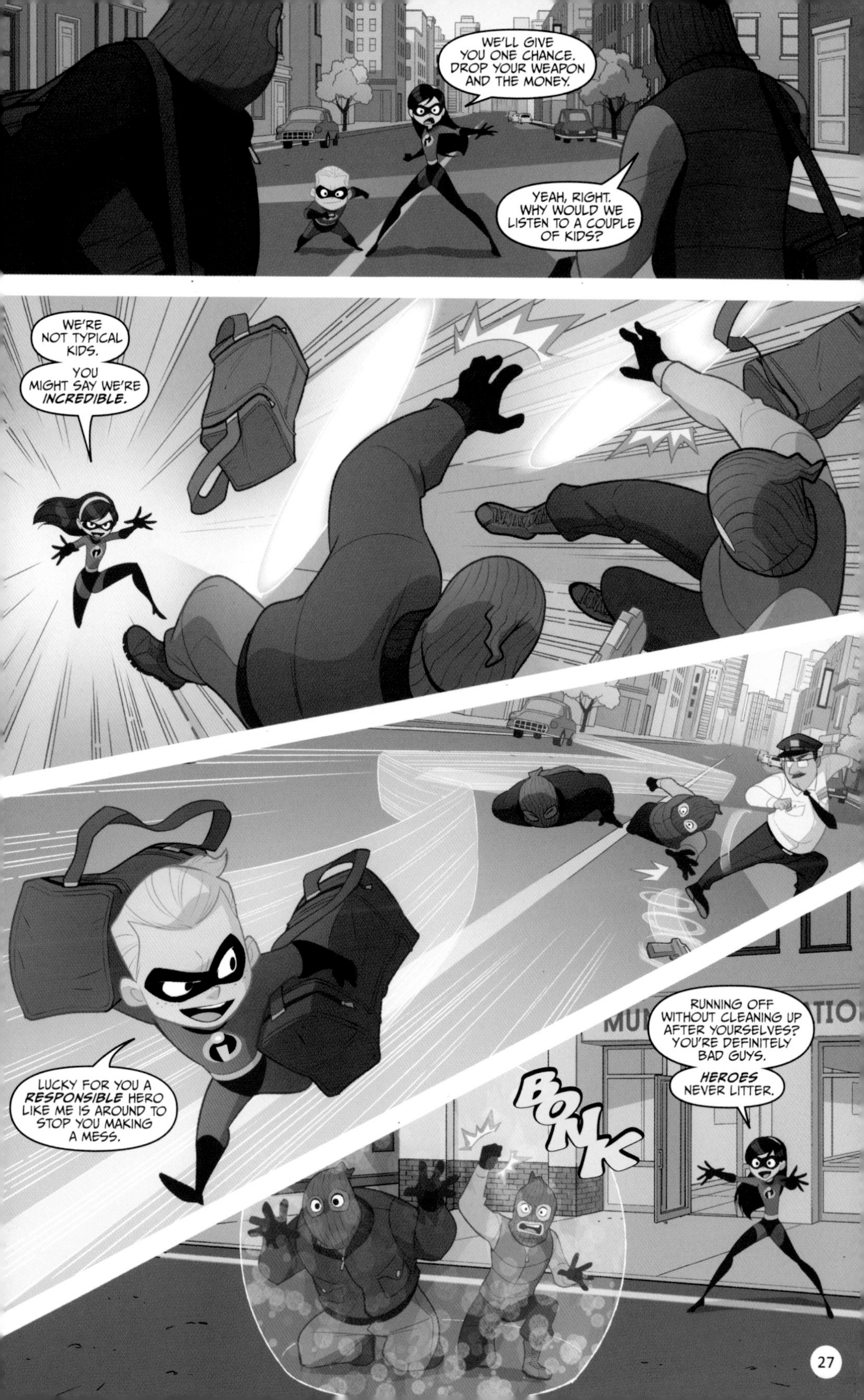
WE'LL GIVE YOU ONE CHANCE. DROP YOUR WEAPON AND THE MONEY.
YEAH, RIGHT. WHY WOULD WE LISTEN TO A COUPLE OF KIDS?
WE'RE NOT TYPICAL KIDS.
YOU MIGHT SAY WE'RE *INCREDIBLE.*
LUCKY FOR YOU A **RESPONSIBLE** HERO LIKE ME IS AROUND TO STOP YOU MAKING A MESS.
RUNNING OFF WITHOUT CLEANING UP AFTER YOURSELVES? YOU'RE DEFINITELY BAD GUYS.
HEROES NEVER LITTER.
BONK

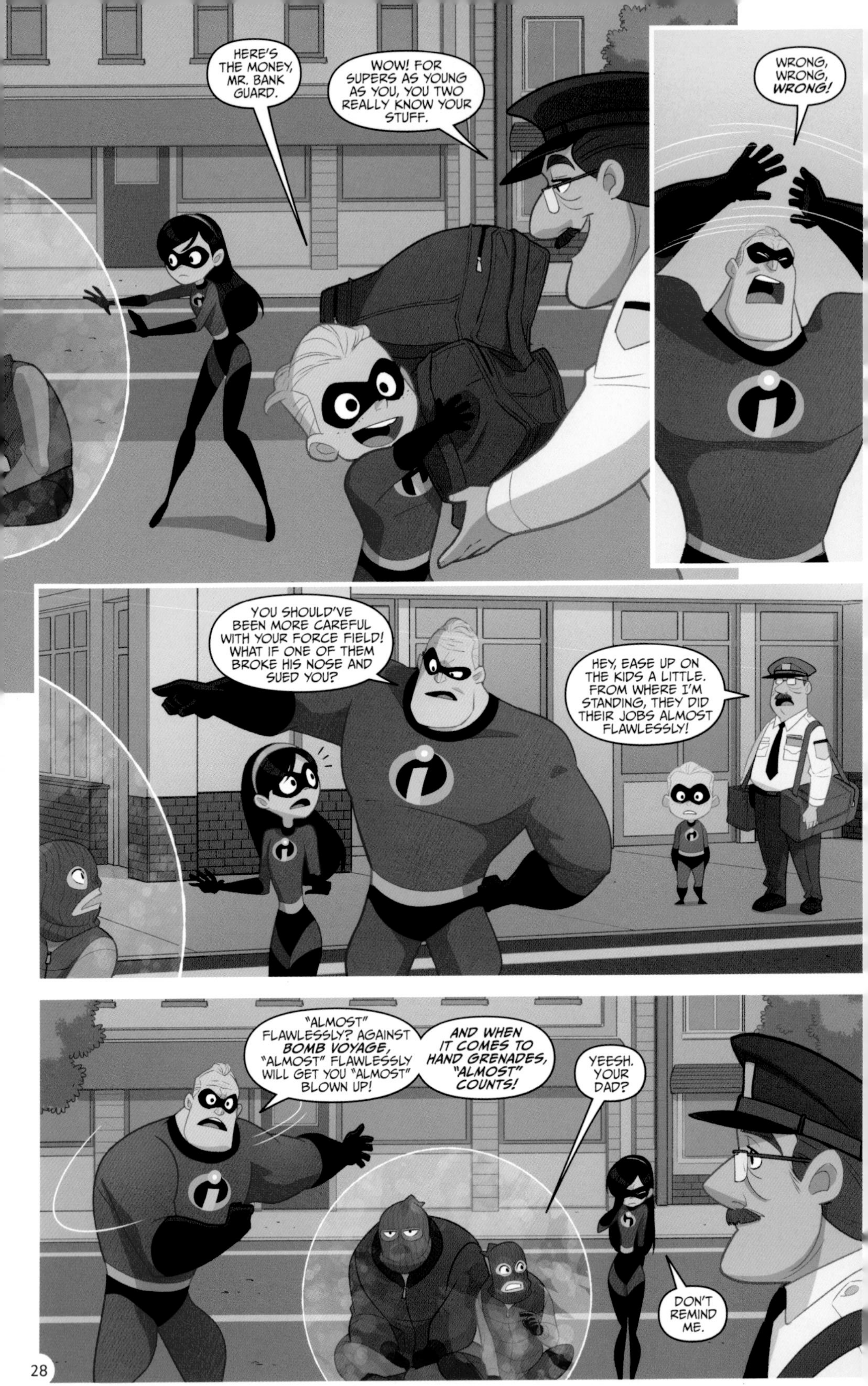
HERE'S THE MONEY, MR. BANK GUARD.
WOW! FOR SUPERS AS YOUNG AS YOU, YOU TWO REALLY KNOW YOUR STUFF.
WRONG, WRONG, **WRONG!**
YOU SHOULD'VE BEEN MORE CAREFUL WITH YOUR FORCE FIELD! WHAT IF ONE OF THEM BROKE HIS NOSE AND SUED YOU?
HEY, EASE UP ON THE KIDS A LITTLE. FROM WHERE I'M STANDING, THEY DID THEIR JOBS ALMOST FLAWLESSLY!
"ALMOST" FLAWLESSLY? AGAINST **BOMB VOYAGE**, "ALMOST" FLAWLESSLY WILL GET YOU "ALMOST" BLOWN UP!
AND WHEN IT COMES TO HAND GRENADES, "ALMOST" COUNTS!
YEESH. YOUR DAD?
DON'T REMIND ME.

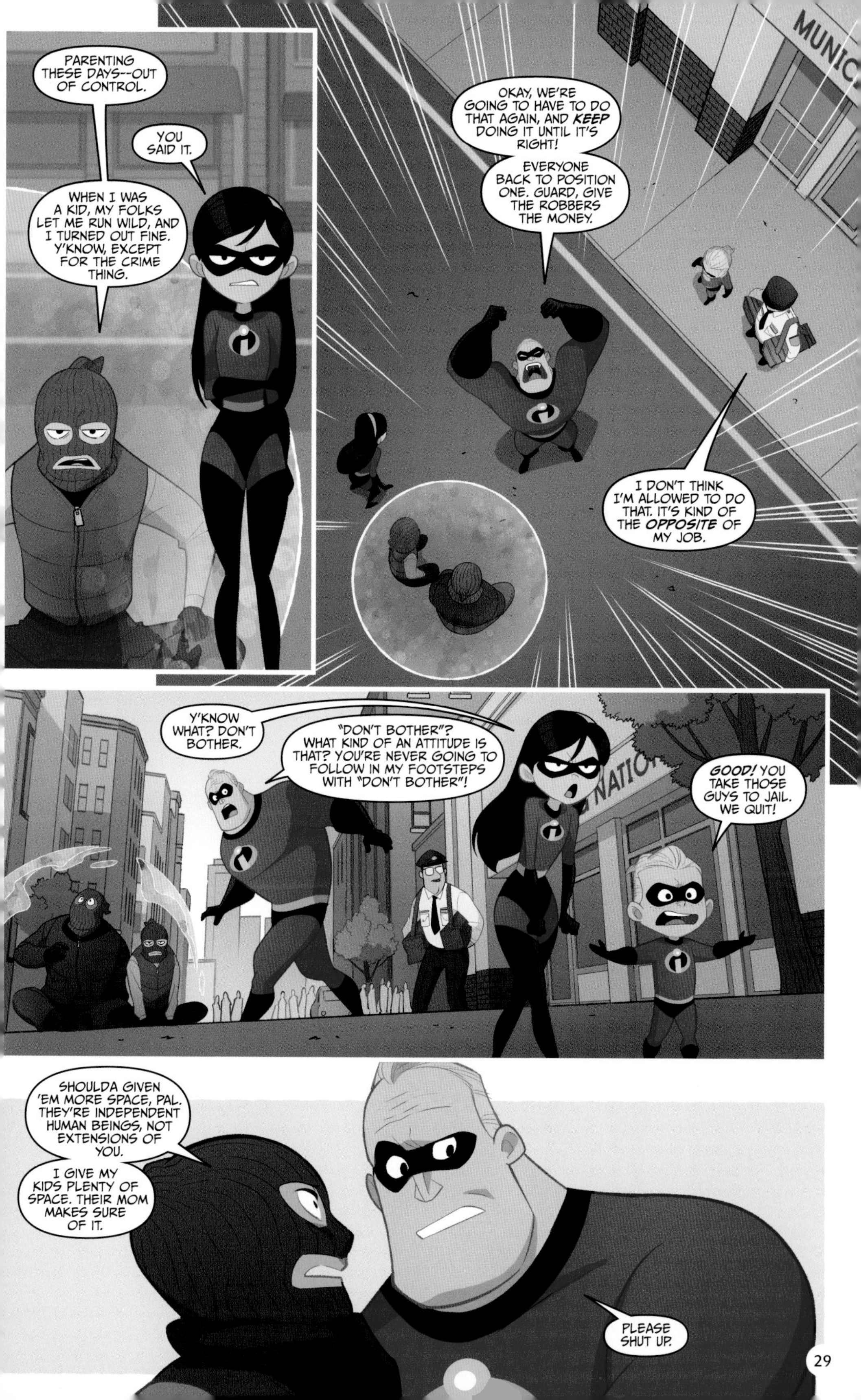
PARENTING THESE DAYS--OUT OF CONTROL.
YOU SAID IT.
WHEN I WAS A KID, MY FOLKS LET ME RUN WILD, AND I TURNED OUT FINE. Y'KNOW, EXCEPT FOR THE CRIME THING.
MUNIC
OKAY, WE'RE GOING TO HAVE TO DO THAT AGAIN, AND KEEP DOING IT UNTIL IT'S RIGHT!
EVERYONE BACK TO POSITION ONE. GUARD, GIVE THE ROBBERS THE MONEY.
I DON'T THINK I'M ALLOWED TO DO THAT. IT'S KIND OF THE OPPOSITE OF MY JOB.
Y'KNOW WHAT? DON'T BOTHER.
"DON'T BOTHER"? WHAT KIND OF AN ATTITUDE IS THAT? YOU'RE NEVER GOING TO FOLLOW IN MY FOOTSTEPS WITH "DON'T BOTHER"!
NATIO
GOOD! YOU TAKE THOSE GUYS TO JAIL. WE QUIT!
SHOULDA GIVEN 'EM MORE SPACE, PAL. THEY'RE INDEPENDENT HUMAN BEINGS, NOT EXTENSIONS OF YOU.
I GIVE MY KIDS PLENTY OF SPACE. THEIR MOM MAKES SURE OF IT.
PLEASE SHUT UP.

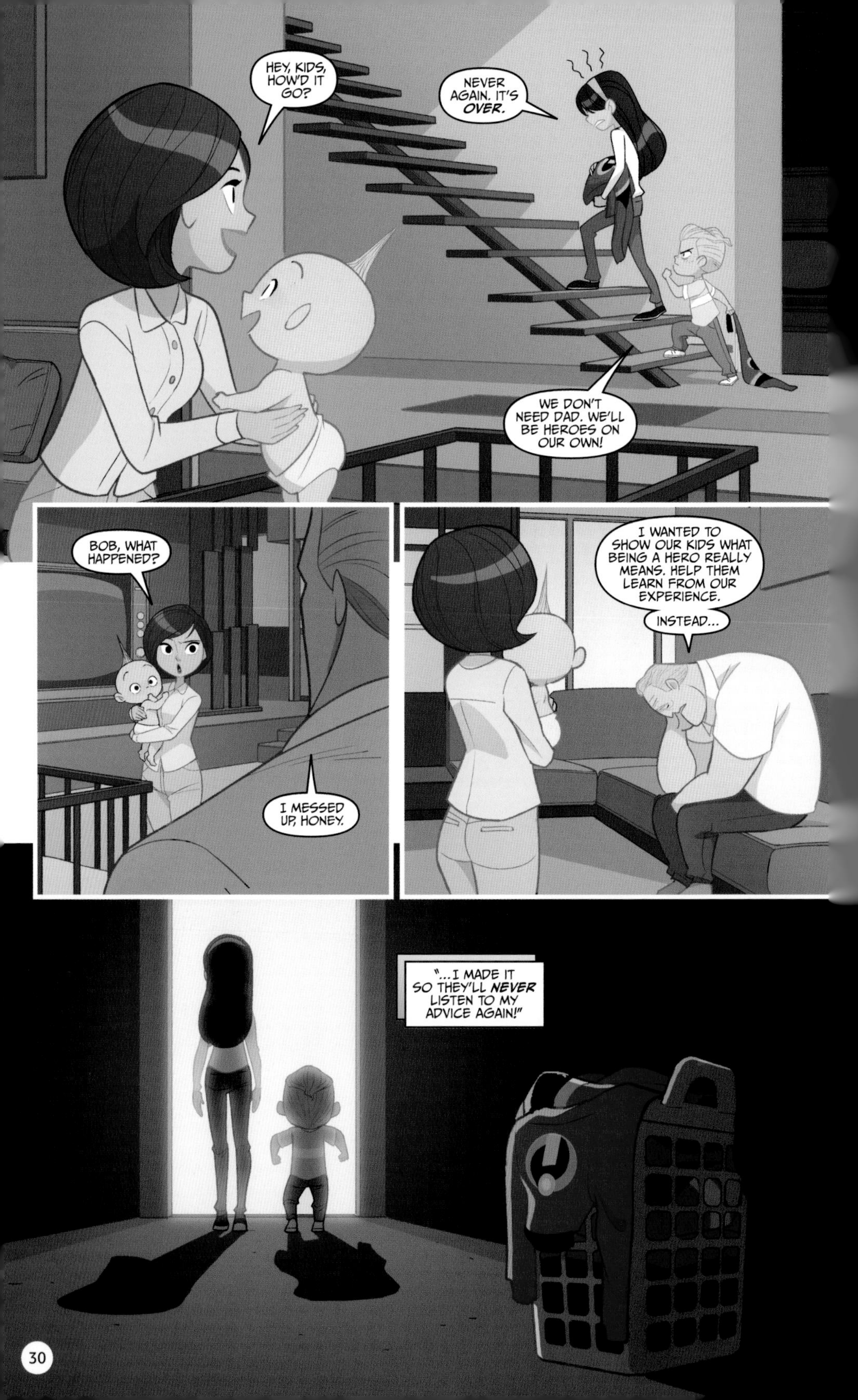
HEY, KIDS, HOW'D IT GO?
NEVER AGAIN. IT'S *OVER.*
WE DON'T NEED DAD. WE'LL BE HEROES ON OUR OWN!
BOB, WHAT HAPPENED?
I MESSED UP, HONEY.
I WANTED TO SHOW OUR KIDS WHAT BEING A HERO REALLY MEANS. HELP THEM LEARN FROM OUR EXPERIENCE.
INSTEAD...
"...I MADE IT SO THEY'LL *NEVER* LISTEN TO MY ADVICE AGAIN!"

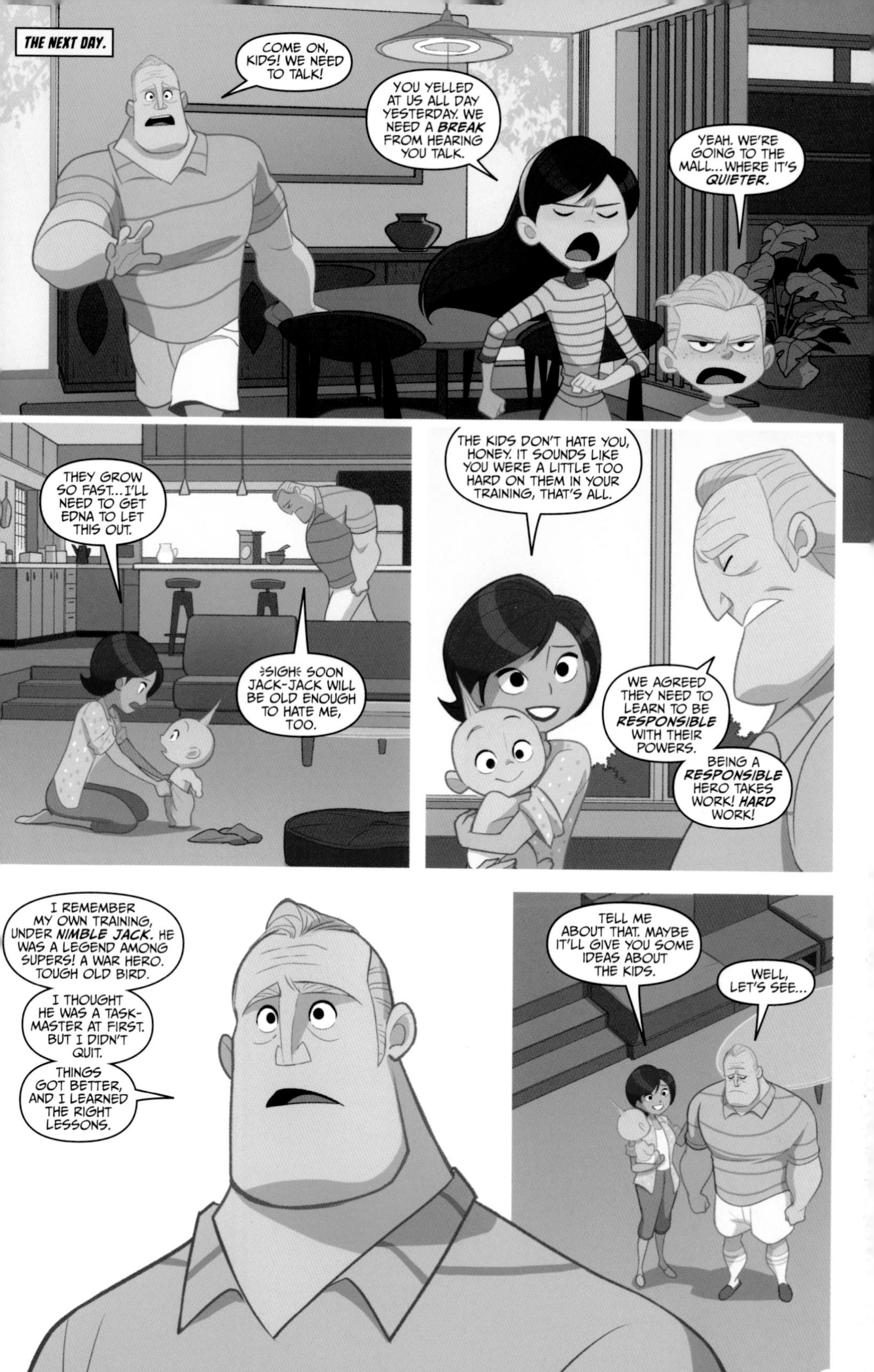
THE NEXT DAY.
COME ON, KIDS! WE NEED TO TALK!
YOU YELLED AT US ALL DAY YESTERDAY. WE NEED A BREAK FROM HEARING YOU TALK.
YEAH. WE'RE GOING TO THE MALL... WHERE IT'S QUIETER.
THEY GROW SO FAST... I'LL NEED TO GET EDNA TO LET THIS OUT.
SIGH SOON JACK-JACK WILL BE OLD ENOUGH TO HATE ME, TOO.
THE KIDS DON'T HATE YOU, HONEY. IT SOUNDS LIKE YOU WERE A LITTLE TOO HARD ON THEM IN YOUR TRAINING, THAT'S ALL.
WE AGREED THEY NEED TO LEARN TO BE RESPONSIBLE WITH THEIR POWERS.
BEING A RESPONSIBLE HERO TAKES WORK! HARD WORK!
I REMEMBER MY OWN TRAINING, UNDER NIMBLE JACK. HE WAS A LEGEND AMONG SUPERS! A WAR HERO. TOUGH OLD BIRD.
I THOUGHT HE WAS A TASK-MASTER AT FIRST. BUT I DIDN'T QUIT.
THINGS GOT BETTER, AND I LEARNED THE RIGHT LESSONS.
TELL ME ABOUT THAT. MAYBE IT'LL GIVE YOU SOME IDEAS ABOUT THE KIDS.
WELL, LET'S SEE...

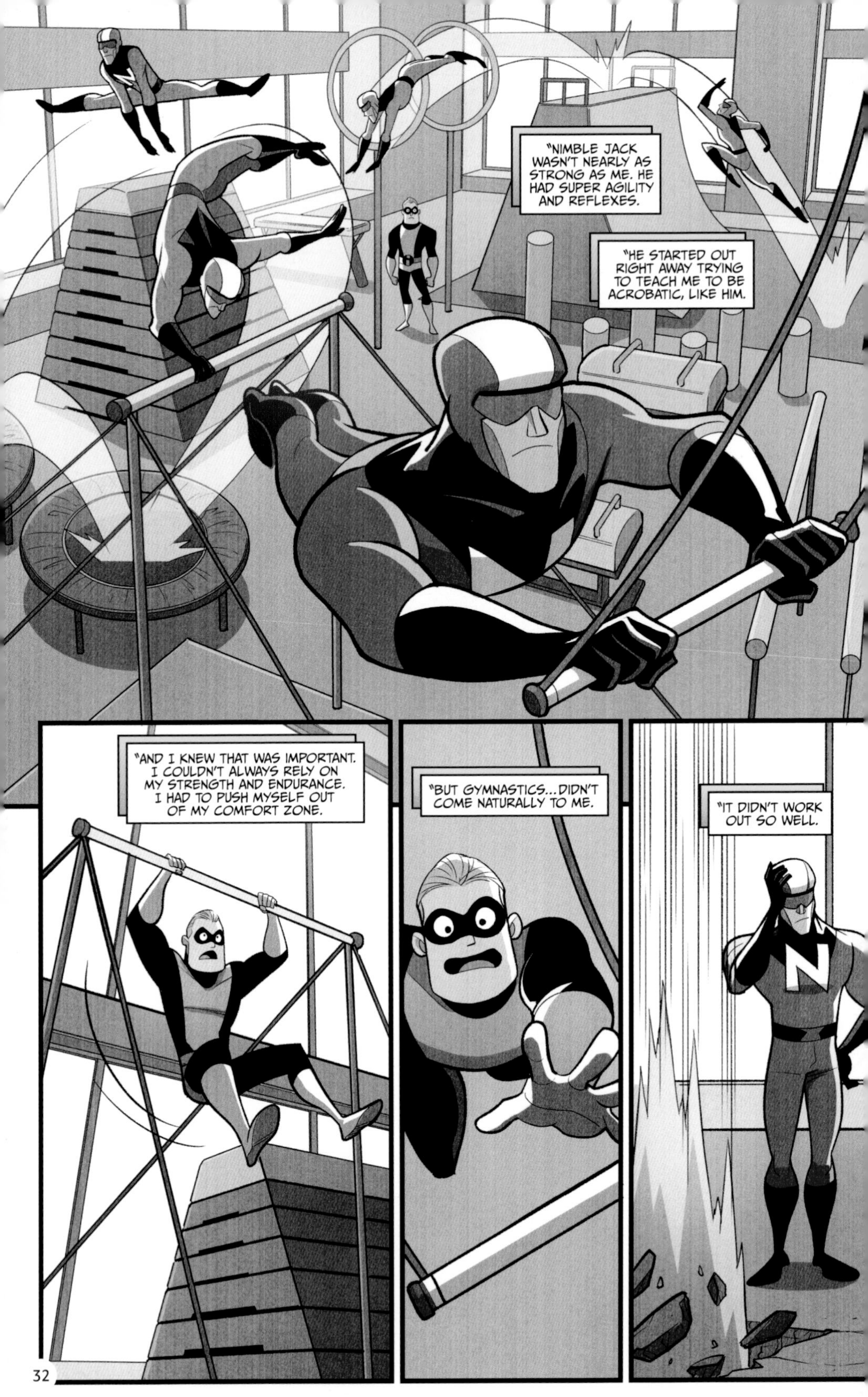
"NIMBLE JACK WASN'T NEARLY AS STRONG AS ME. HE HAD SUPER AGILITY AND REFLEXES.
"HE STARTED OUT RIGHT AWAY TRYING TO TEACH ME TO BE ACROBATIC, LIKE HIM.
"AND I KNEW THAT WAS IMPORTANT. I COULDN'T ALWAYS RELY ON MY STRENGTH AND ENDURANCE. I HAD TO PUSH MYSELF OUT OF MY COMFORT ZONE.
"BUT GYMNASTICS...DIDN'T COME NATURALLY TO ME.
"IT DIDN'T WORK OUT SO WELL.

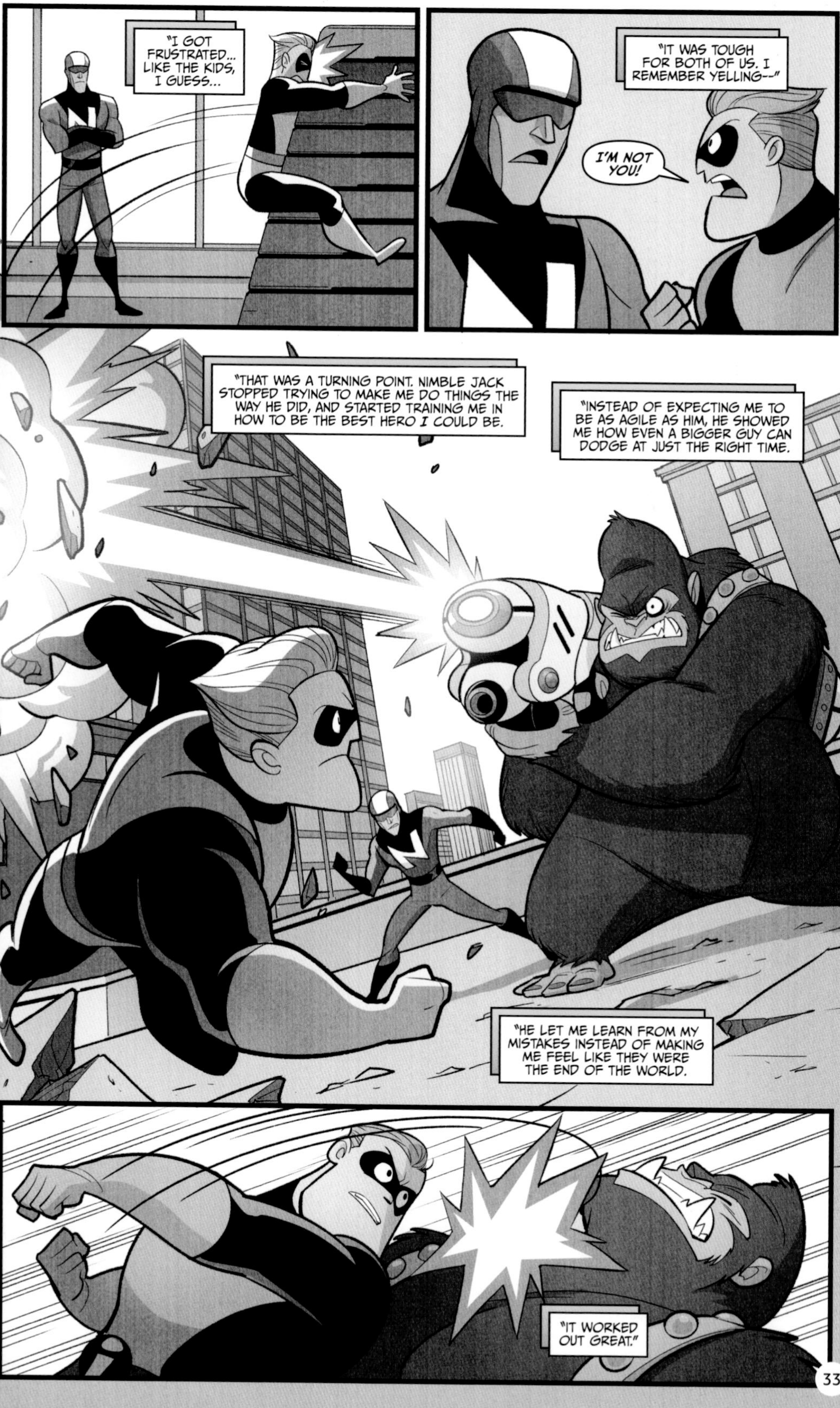
"I GOT FRUSTRATED... LIKE THE KIDS, I GUESS...
"IT WAS TOUGH FOR BOTH OF US. I REMEMBER YELLING--"
I'M NOT YOU!
"THAT WAS A TURNING POINT. NIMBLE JACK STOPPED TRYING TO MAKE ME DO THINGS THE WAY HE DID, AND STARTED TRAINING ME IN HOW TO BE THE BEST HERO I COULD BE.
"INSTEAD OF EXPECTING ME TO BE AS AGILE AS HIM, HE SHOWED ME HOW EVEN A BIGGER GUY CAN DODGE AT JUST THE RIGHT TIME.
"HE LET ME LEARN FROM MY MISTAKES INSTEAD OF MAKING ME FEEL LIKE THEY WERE THE END OF THE WORLD.
"IT WORKED OUT GREAT."

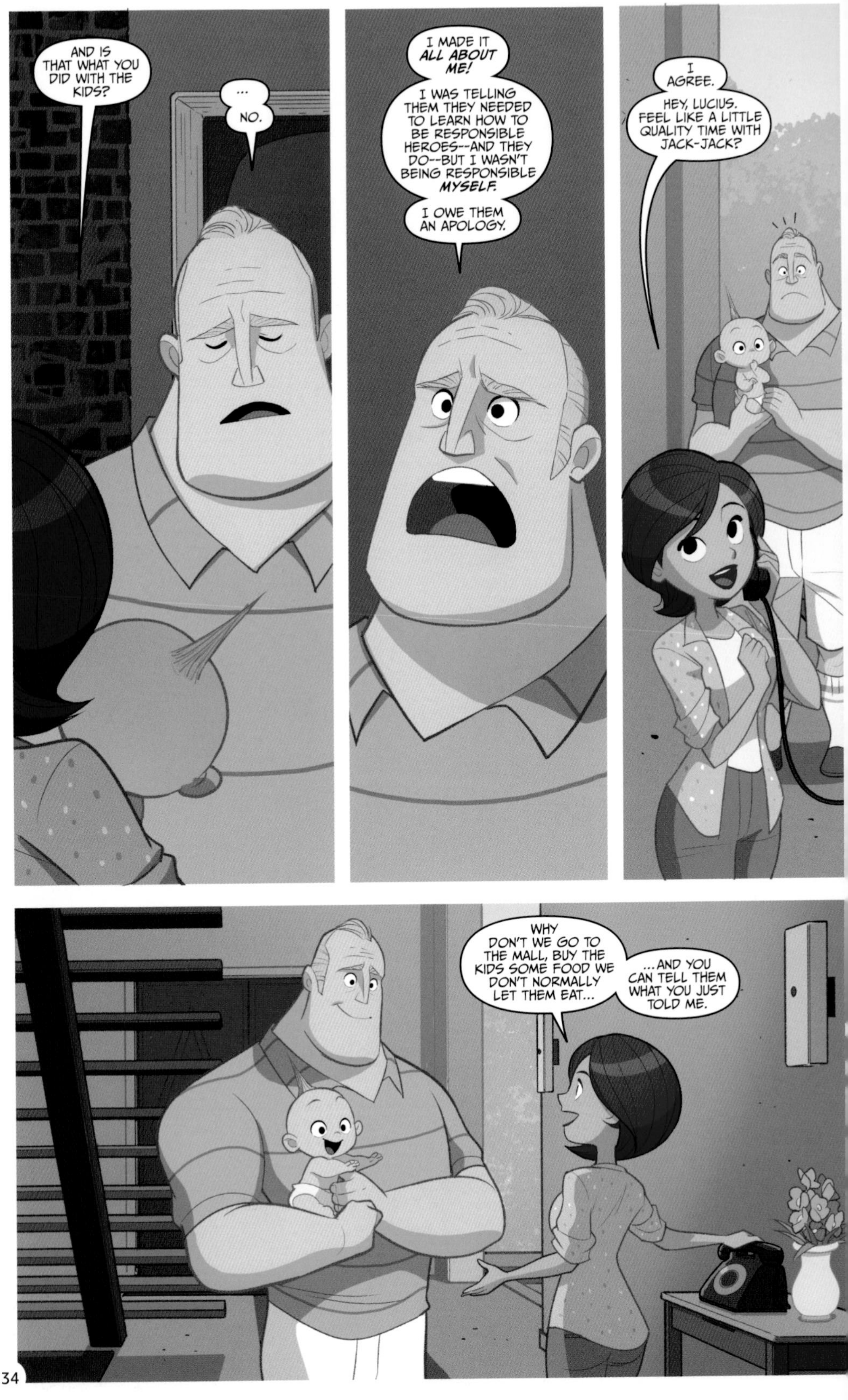

AND IS THAT WHAT YOU DID WITH THE KIDS?
...
NO.
I MADE IT ALL ABOUT ME!
I WAS TELLING THEM THEY NEEDED TO LEARN HOW TO BE RESPONSIBLE HEROES--AND THEY DO--BUT I WASN'T BEING RESPONSIBLE MYSELF.
I OWE THEM AN APOLOGY.
I AGREE.
HEY, LUCIUS. FEEL LIKE A LITTLE QUALITY TIME WITH JACK-JACK?
WHY DON'T WE GO TO THE MALL, BUY THE KIDS SOME FOOD WE DON'T NORMALLY LET THEM EAT...
...AND YOU CAN TELL THEM WHAT YOU JUST TOLD ME.

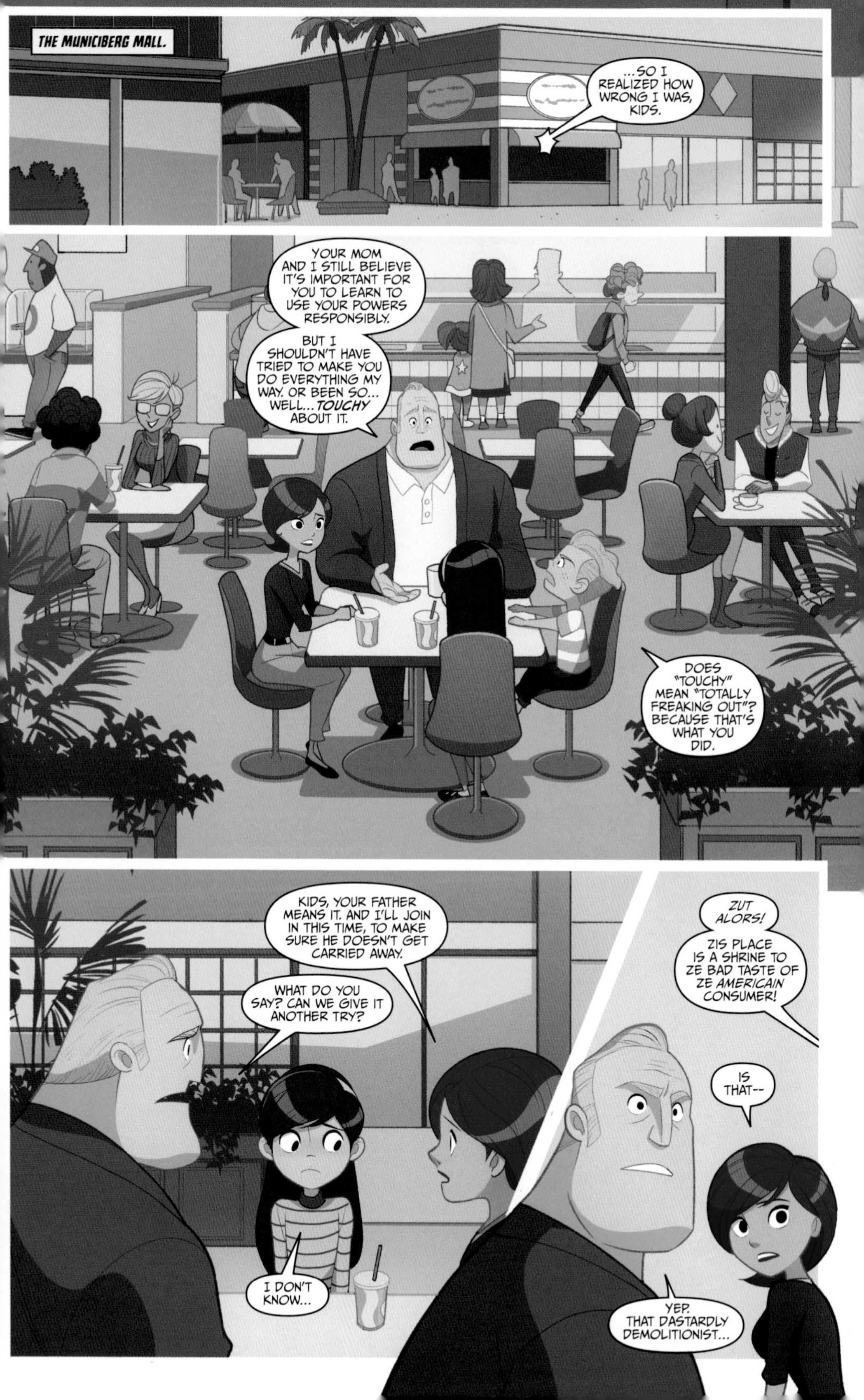
THE MUNICIBERG MALL.
...SO I REALIZED HOW WRONG I WAS, KIDS.
YOUR MOM AND I STILL BELIEVE IT'S IMPORTANT FOR YOU TO LEARN TO USE YOUR POWERS RESPONSIBLY.
BUT I SHOULDN'T HAVE TRIED TO MAKE YOU DO EVERYTHING MY WAY. OR BEEN SO... WELL...TOUCHY ABOUT IT.
DOES "TOUCHY" MEAN "TOTALLY FREAKING OUT"? BECAUSE THAT'S WHAT YOU DID.
KIDS, YOUR FATHER MEANS IT. AND I'LL JOIN IN THIS TIME, TO MAKE SURE HE DOESN'T GET CARRIED AWAY.
WHAT DO YOU SAY? CAN WE GIVE IT ANOTHER TRY?
I DON'T KNOW...
ZUT ALORS!
ZIS PLACE IS A SHRINE TO ZE BAD TASTE OF ZE AMERICAIN CONSUMER!
IS THAT--
YEP. THAT DASTARDLY DEMOLITIONIST...

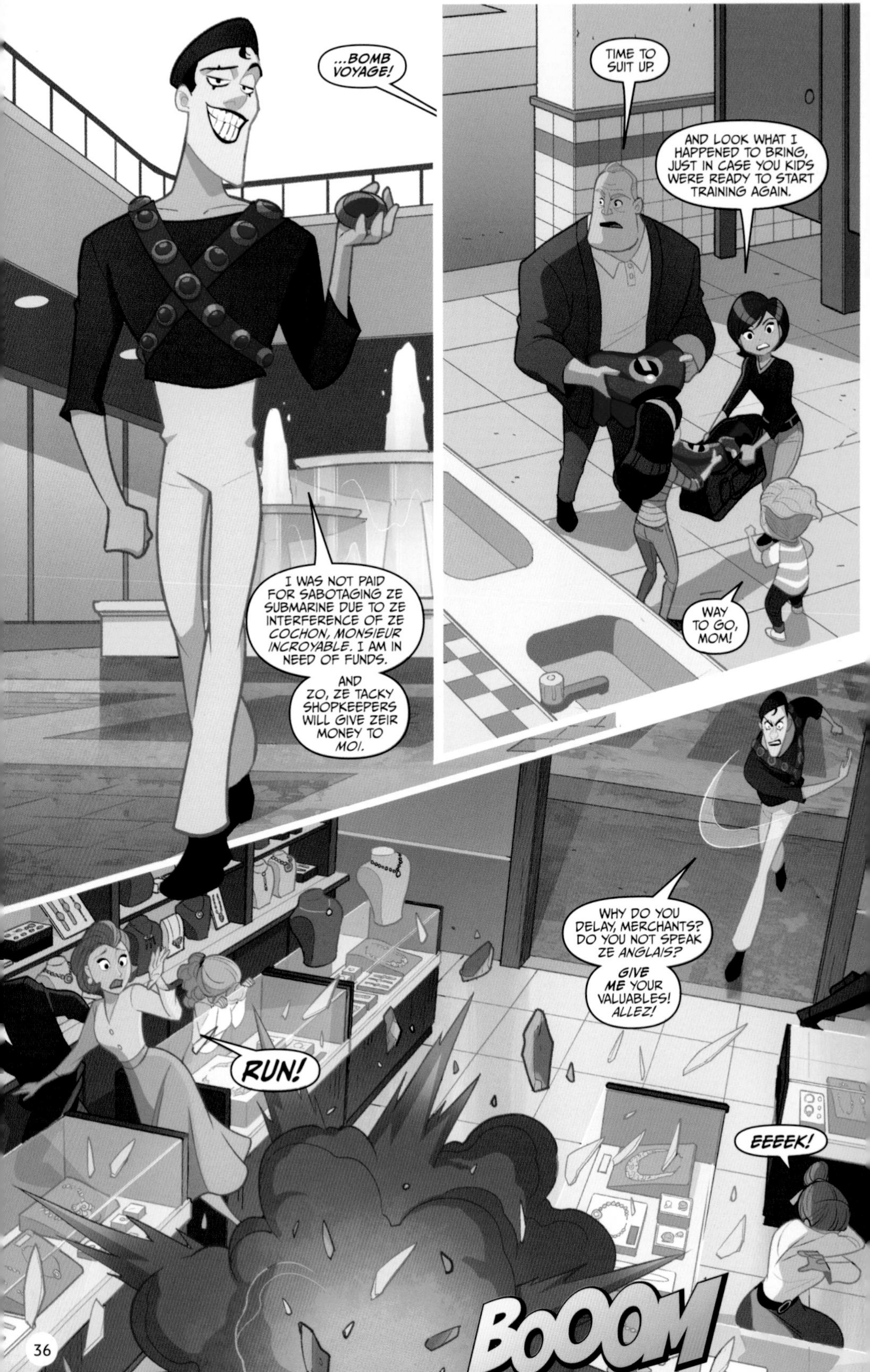
...BOMB VOYAGE!
I WAS NOT PAID FOR SABOTAGING ZE SUBMARINE DUE TO ZE INTERFERENCE OF ZE COCHON, MONSIEUR INCROYABLE. I AM IN NEED OF FUNDS.
AND ZO, ZE TACKY SHOPKEEPERS WILL GIVE ZEIR MONEY TO MOI!
TIME TO SUIT UP.
AND LOOK WHAT I HAPPENED TO BRING, JUST IN CASE YOU KIDS WERE READY TO START TRAINING AGAIN.
WAY TO GO, MOM!
WHY DO YOU DELAY, MERCHANTS? DO YOU NOT SPEAK ZE ANGLAIS?
GIVE ME YOUR VALUABLES! ALLEZ!
RUN!
EEEEK!
BOOOM

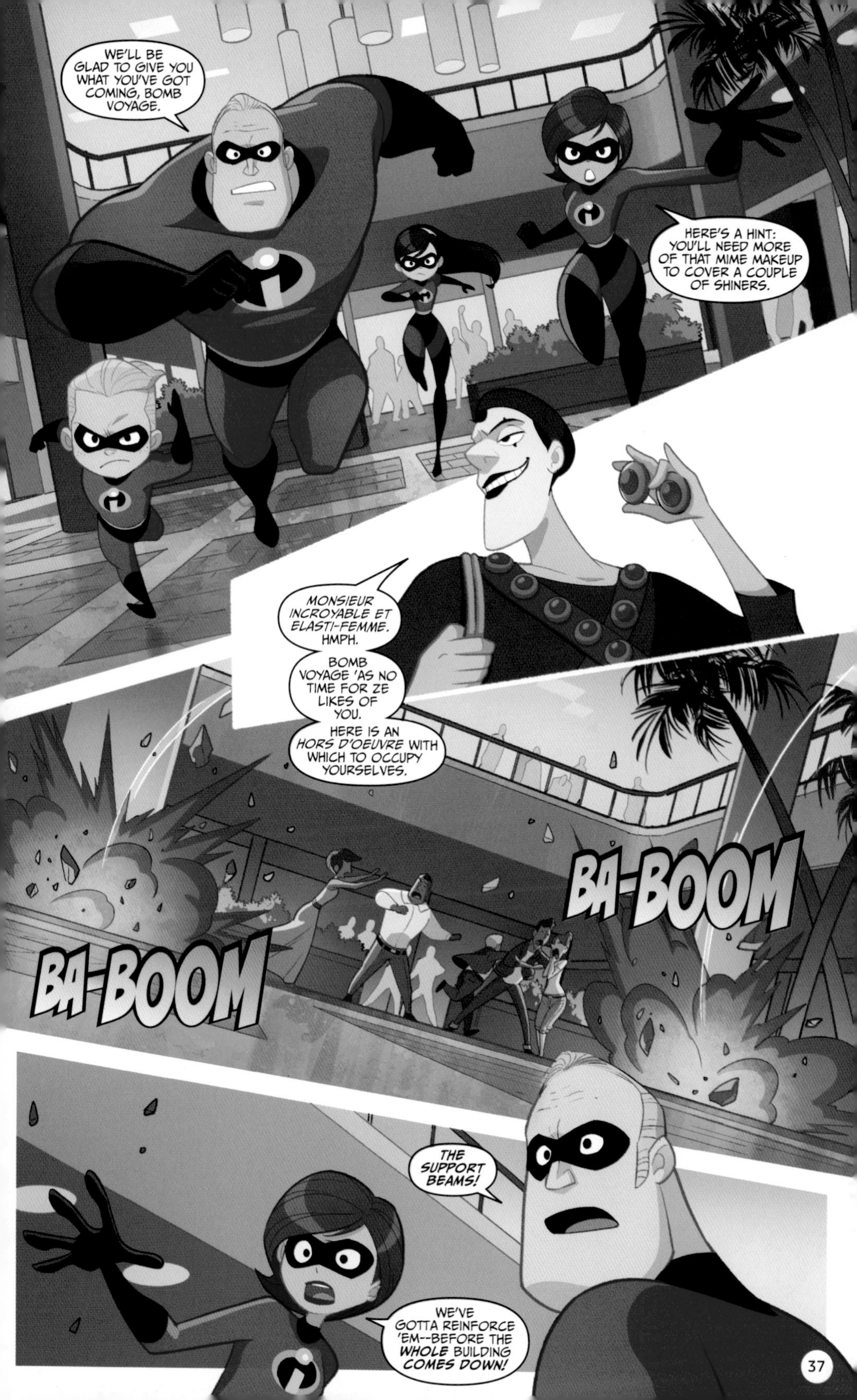
WE'LL BE GLAD TO GIVE YOU WHAT YOU'VE GOT COMING, BOMB VOYAGE.
HERE'S A HINT: YOU'LL NEED MORE OF THAT MIME MAKEUP TO COVER A COUPLE OF SHINERS.
MONSIEUR INCROYABLE ET ELASTI-FEMME. HMPH.
BOMB VOYAGE 'AS NO TIME FOR ZE LIKES OF YOU.
HERE IS AN HORS D'OEUVRE WITH WHICH TO OCCUPY YOURSELVES.
BA-BOOM
BA-BOOM
THE SUPPORT BEAMS!
WE'VE GOTTA REINFORCE 'EM--BEFORE THE WHOLE BUILDING COMES DOWN!

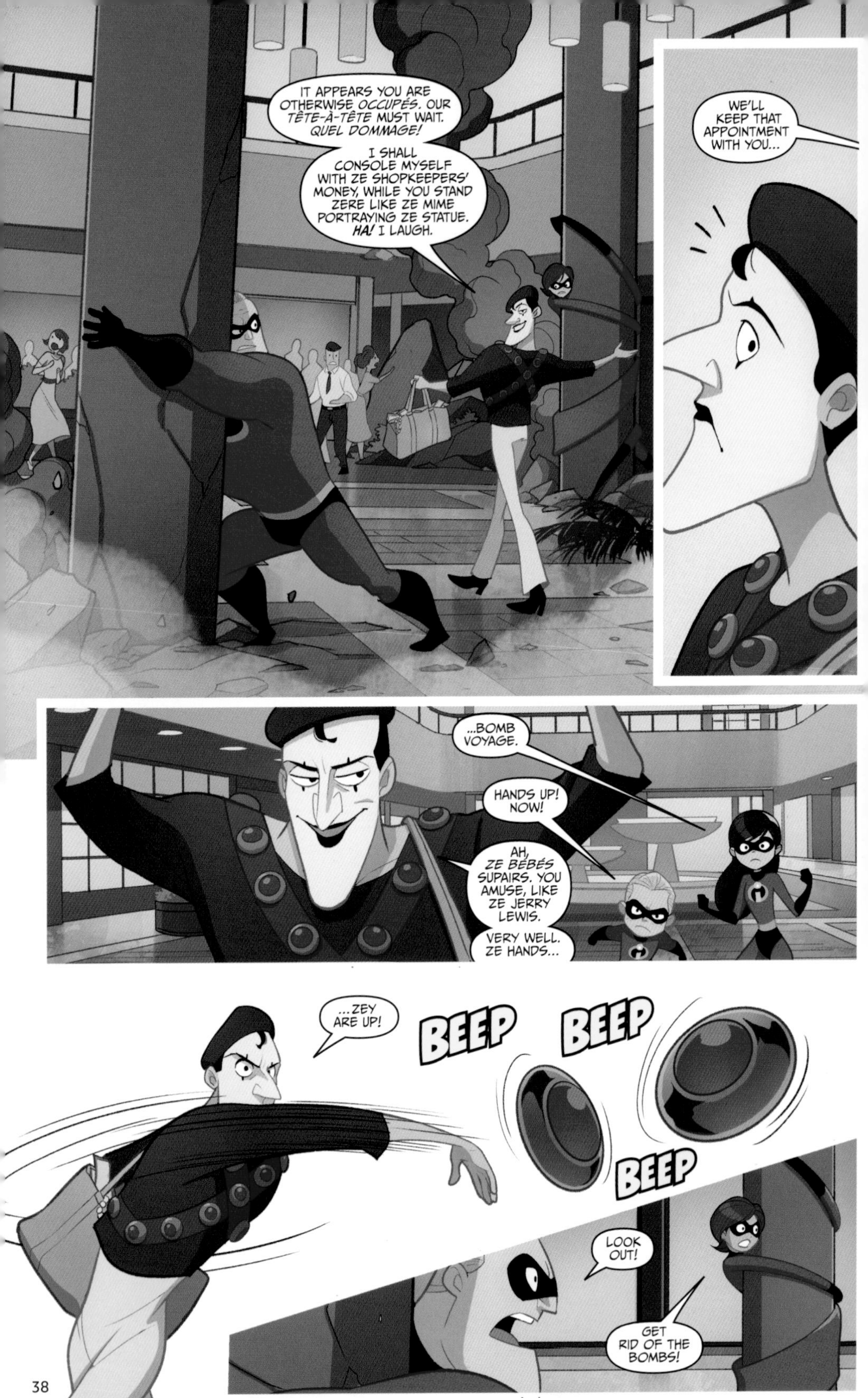
IT APPEARS YOU ARE OTHERWISE *OCCUPÉS*. OUR *TÊTE-À-TÊTE* MUST WAIT. *QUEL DOMMAGE!*
I SHALL CONSOLE MYSELF WITH ZE SHOPKEEPERS' MONEY, WHILE YOU STAND ZERE LIKE ZE MIME PORTRAYING ZE STATUE. ***HA!*** I LAUGH.
WE'LL KEEP THAT APPOINTMENT WITH YOU...
...BOMB VOYAGE.
HANDS UP! NOW!
AH, *ZE BÉBÉS* SUPAIRS. YOU AMUSE, LIKE ZE JERRY LEWIS.
VERY WELL. ZE HANDS...
...ZEY ARE UP!
BEEP
BEEP
BEEP
LOOK OUT!
GET RID OF THE BOMBS!

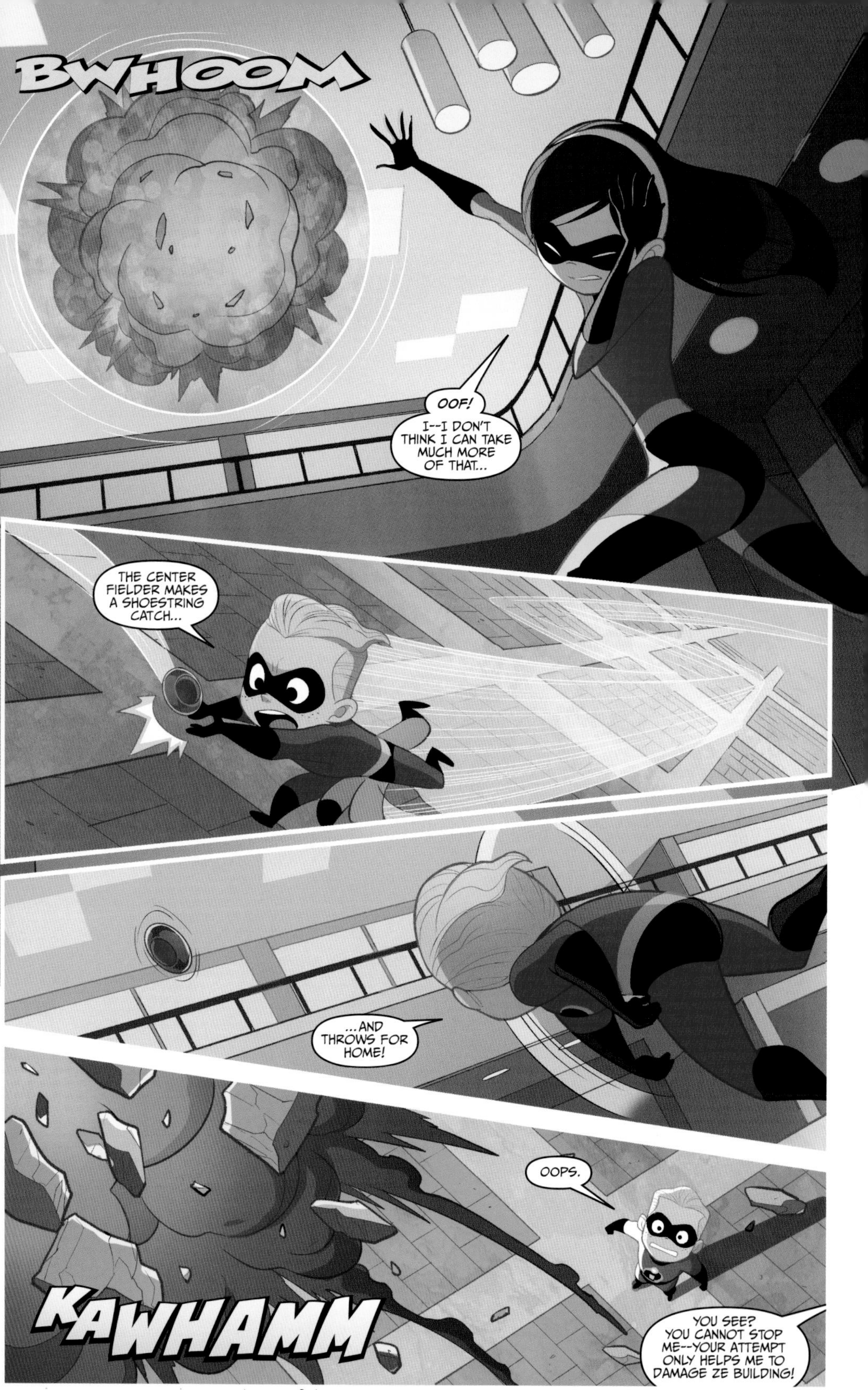
BWHOOM
OOF!
I--I DON'T THINK I CAN TAKE MUCH MORE OF THAT...
THE CENTER FIELDER MAKES A SHOESTRING CATCH...
...AND THROWS FOR HOME!
KAWHAMM
OOPS.
YOU SEE? YOU CANNOT STOP ME--YOUR ATTEMPT ONLY HELPS ME TO DAMAGE ZE BUILDING!

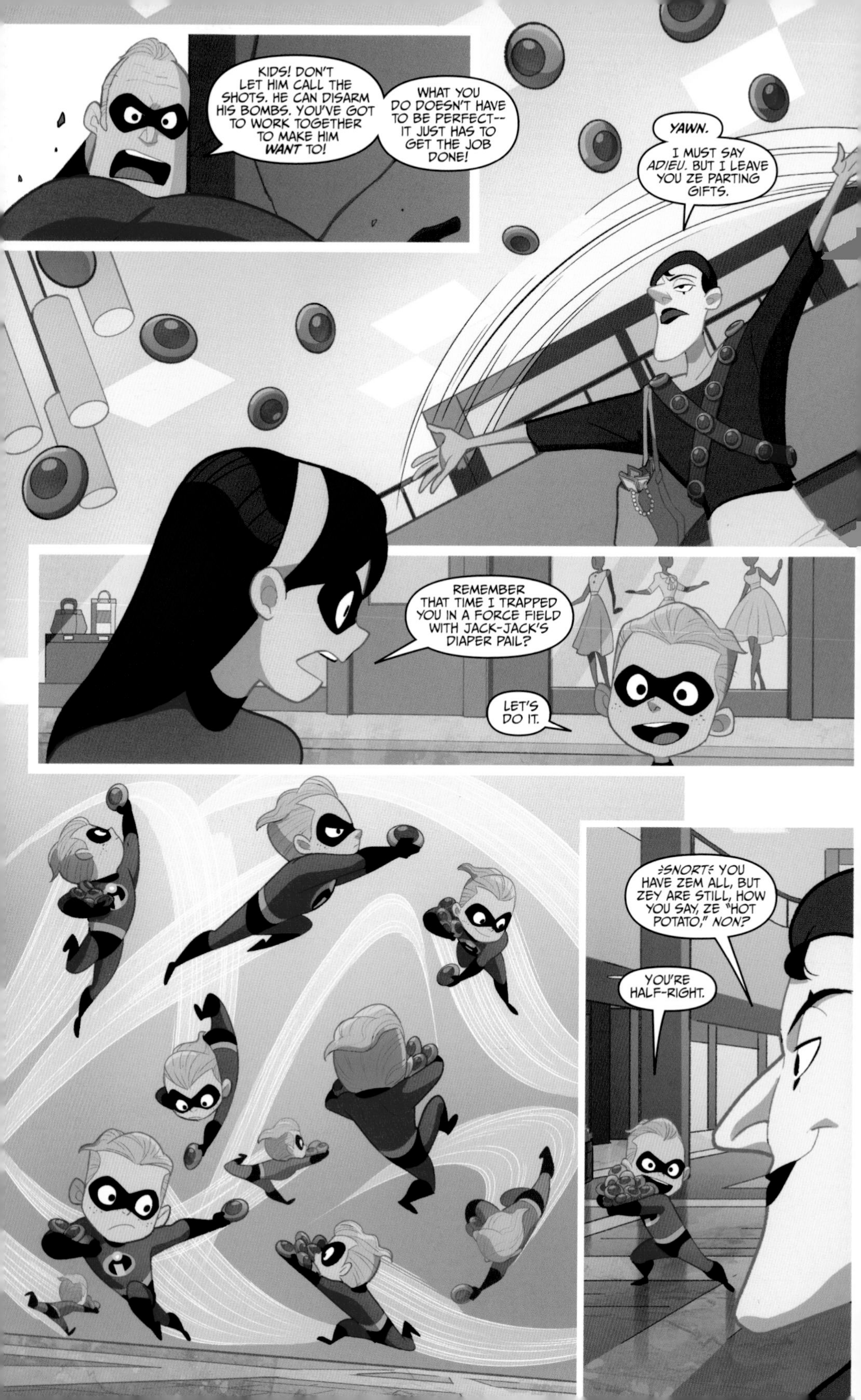
KIDS! DON'T LET HIM CALL THE SHOTS. HE CAN DISARM HIS BOMBS. YOU'VE GOT TO WORK TOGETHER TO MAKE HIM *WANT* TO!
WHAT YOU DO DOESN'T HAVE TO BE PERFECT-- IT JUST HAS TO GET THE JOB DONE!
YAWN.
I MUST SAY *ADIEU*. BUT I LEAVE YOU ZE PARTING GIFTS.
REMEMBER THAT TIME I TRAPPED YOU IN A FORCE FIELD WITH JACK-JACK'S DIAPER PAIL?
LET'S DO IT.
SNORT YOU HAVE ZEM ALL, BUT ZEY ARE STILL, HOW YOU SAY, ZE "HOT POTATO," *NON?*
YOU'RE HALF-RIGHT.

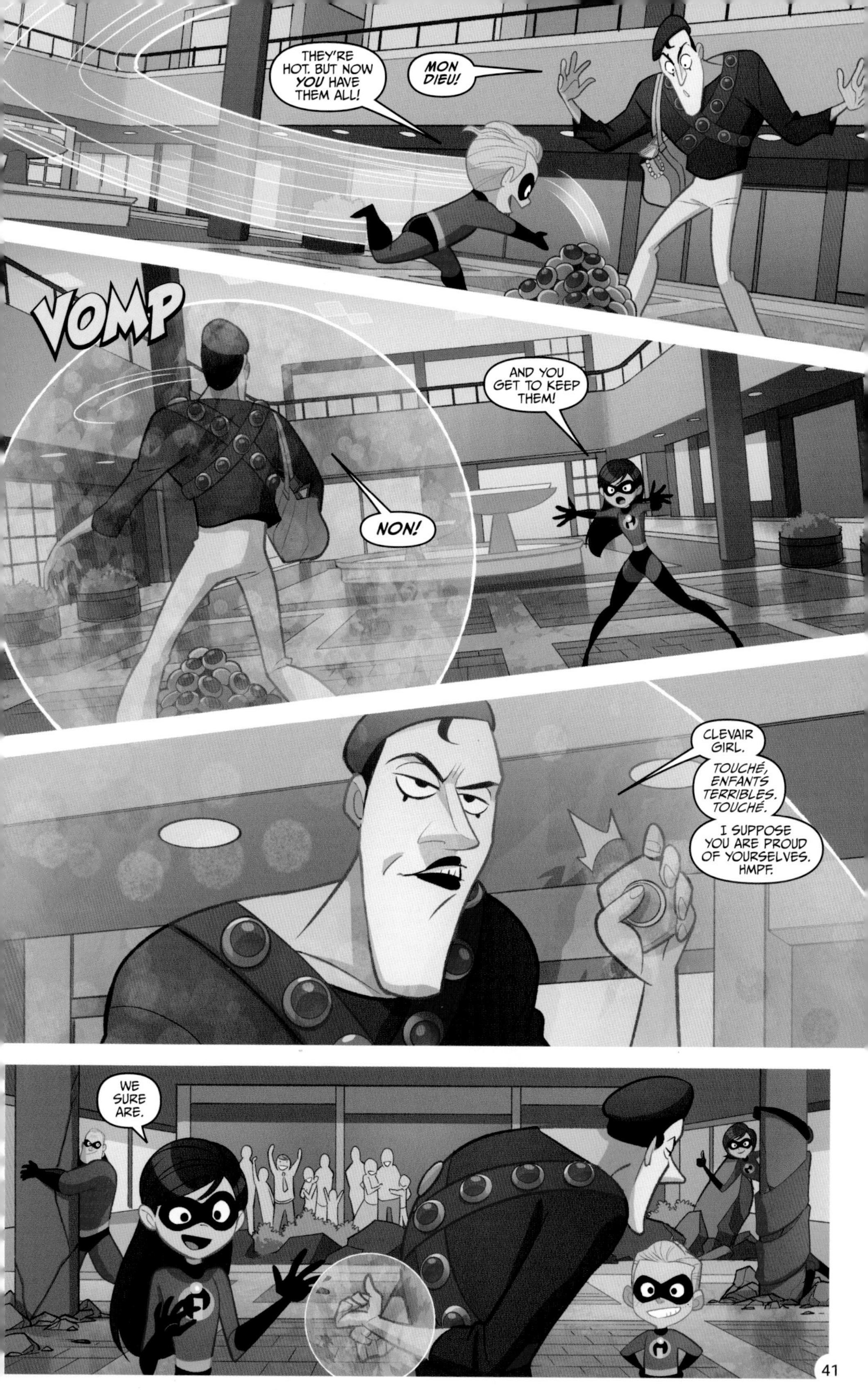
THEY'RE HOT. BUT NOW YOU HAVE THEM ALL!
MON DIEU!
VOMP
AND YOU GET TO KEEP THEM!
NON!
CLEVAIR GIRL.
TOUCHÉ, ENFANTS TERRIBLES. TOUCHÉ.
I SUPPOSE YOU ARE PROUD OF YOURSELVES. HMPF.
WE SURE ARE.

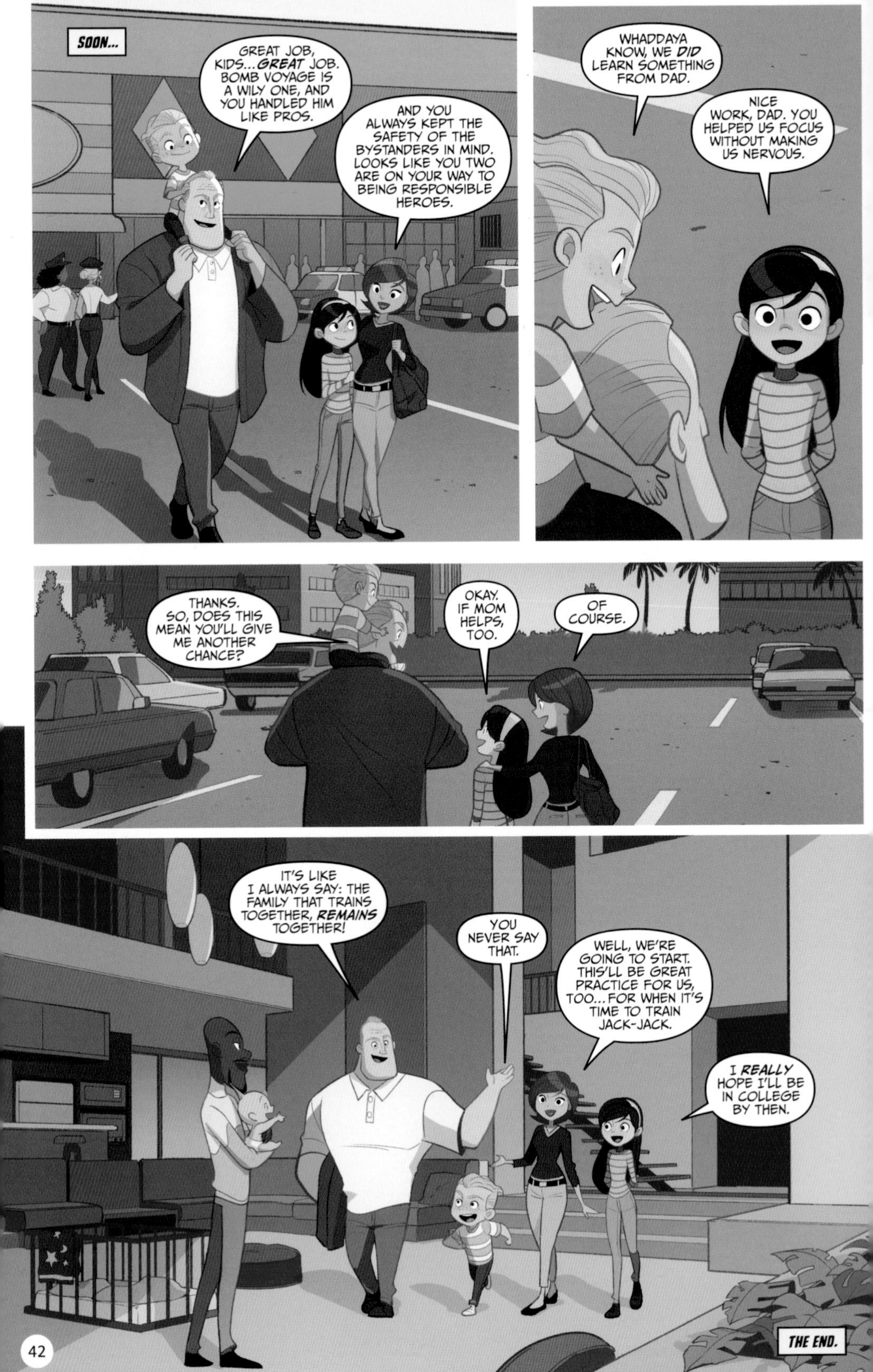
SOON...
GREAT JOB, KIDS...GREAT JOB. BOMB VOYAGE IS A WILY ONE, AND YOU HANDLED HIM LIKE PROS.
AND YOU ALWAYS KEPT THE SAFETY OF THE BYSTANDERS IN MIND. LOOKS LIKE YOU TWO ARE ON YOUR WAY TO BEING RESPONSIBLE HEROES.
WHADDAYA KNOW, WE DID LEARN SOMETHING FROM DAD.
NICE WORK, DAD. YOU HELPED US FOCUS WITHOUT MAKING US NERVOUS.
THANKS. SO, DOES THIS MEAN YOU'LL GIVE ME ANOTHER CHANCE?
OKAY. IF MOM HELPS, TOO.
OF COURSE.
IT'S LIKE I ALWAYS SAY: THE FAMILY THAT TRAINS TOGETHER, REMAINS TOGETHER!
YOU NEVER SAY THAT.
WELL, WE'RE GOING TO START. THIS'LL BE GREAT PRACTICE FOR US, TOO...FOR WHEN IT'S TIME TO TRAIN JACK-JACK.
I REALLY HOPE I'LL BE IN COLLEGE BY THEN.
THE END.

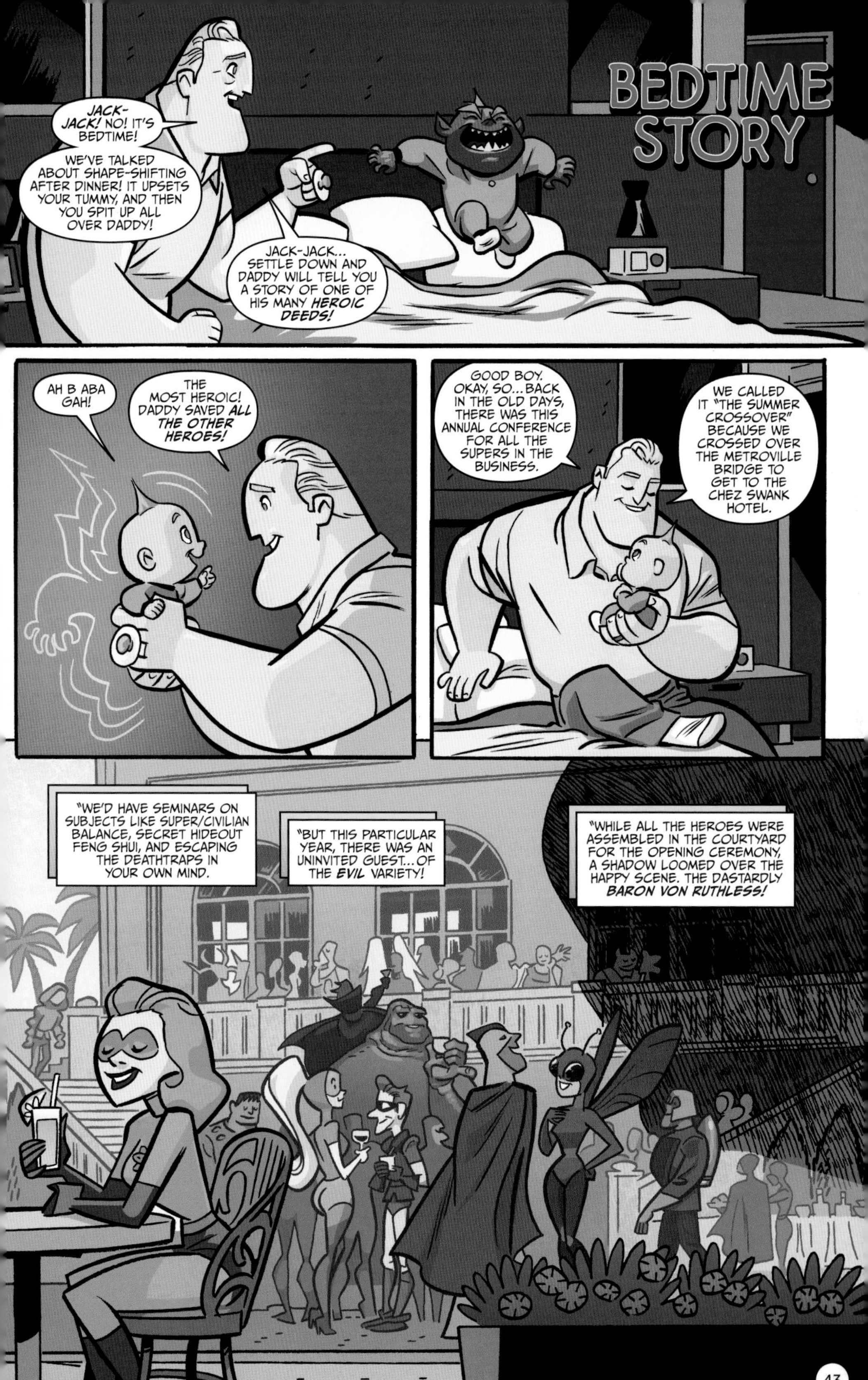
BEDTIME STORY
JACK-JACK! NO! IT'S BEDTIME!
WE'VE TALKED ABOUT SHAPE-SHIFTING AFTER DINNER! IT UPSETS YOUR TUMMY, AND THEN YOU SPIT UP ALL OVER DADDY!
JACK-JACK... SETTLE DOWN AND DADDY WILL TELL YOU A STORY OF ONE OF HIS MANY HEROIC DEEDS!
AH B ABA GAH!
THE MOST HEROIC! DADDY SAVED ALL THE OTHER HEROES!
GOOD BOY. OKAY, SO...BACK IN THE OLD DAYS, THERE WAS THIS ANNUAL CONFERENCE FOR ALL THE SUPERS IN THE BUSINESS.
WE CALLED IT "THE SUMMER CROSSOVER" BECAUSE WE CROSSED OVER THE METROVILLE BRIDGE TO GET TO THE CHEZ SWANK HOTEL.
"WE'D HAVE SEMINARS ON SUBJECTS LIKE SUPER/CIVILIAN BALANCE, SECRET HIDEOUT FENG SHUI, AND ESCAPING THE DEATHTRAPS IN YOUR OWN MIND.
"BUT THIS PARTICULAR YEAR, THERE WAS AN UNINVITED GUEST...OF THE EVIL VARIETY!
"WHILE ALL THE HEROES WERE ASSEMBLED IN THE COURTYARD FOR THE OPENING CEREMONY, A SHADOW LOOMED OVER THE HAPPY SCENE. THE DASTARDLY BARON VON RUTHLESS!

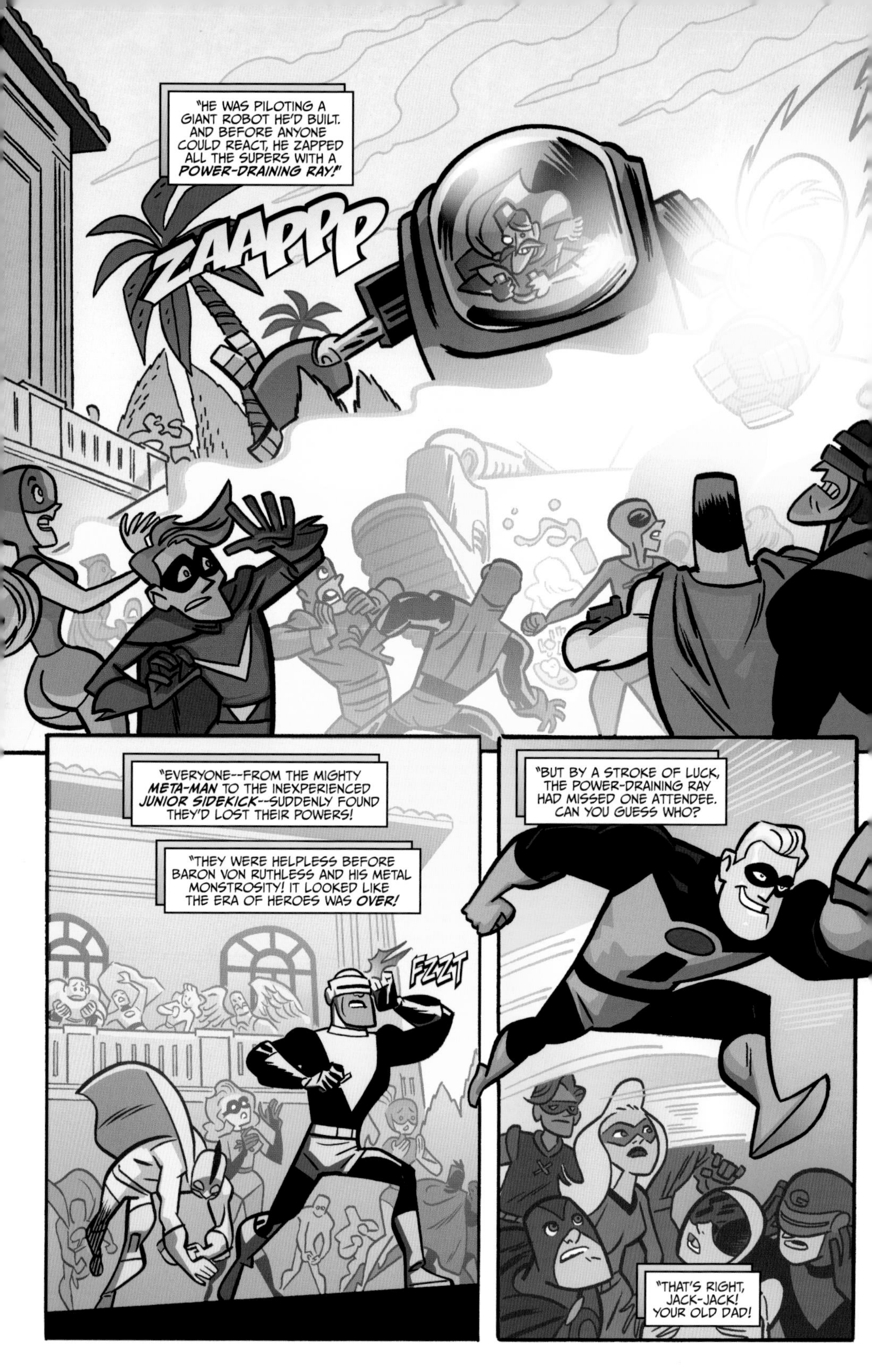

"HE WAS PILOTING A GIANT ROBOT HE'D BUILT. AND BEFORE ANYONE COULD REACT, HE ZAPPED ALL THE SUPERS WITH A POWER-DRAINING RAY!"
ZAAPPP
"EVERYONE--FROM THE MIGHTY META-MAN TO THE INEXPERIENCED JUNIOR SIDEKICK--SUDDENLY FOUND THEY'D LOST THEIR POWERS!
"THEY WERE HELPLESS BEFORE BARON VON RUTHLESS AND HIS METAL MONSTROSITY! IT LOOKED LIKE THE ERA OF HEROES WAS OVER!
FZZT
"BUT BY A STROKE OF LUCK, THE POWER-DRAINING RAY HAD MISSED ONE ATTENDEE. CAN YOU GUESS WHO?
"THAT'S RIGHT, JACK-JACK! YOUR OLD DAD!

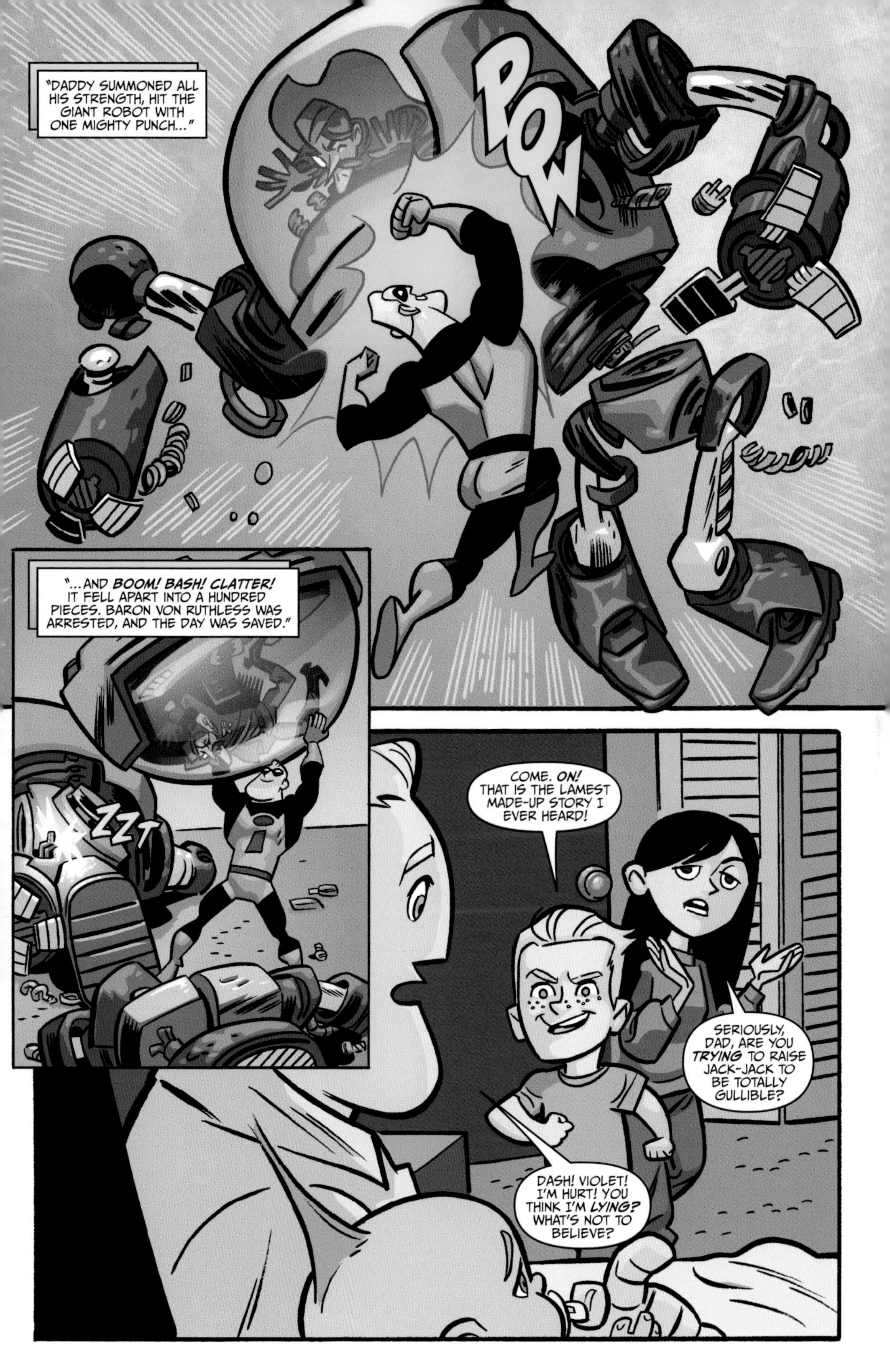
"DADDY SUMMONED ALL HIS STRENGTH, HIT THE GIANT ROBOT WITH ONE MIGHTY PUNCH..."
POW
"...AND BOOM! BASH! CLATTER! IT FELL APART INTO A HUNDRED PIECES. BARON VON RUTHLESS WAS ARRESTED, AND THE DAY WAS SAVED."
ZZZT
COME. ON! THAT IS THE LAMEST MADE-UP STORY I EVER HEARD!
SERIOUSLY, DAD, ARE YOU TRYING TO RAISE JACK-JACK TO BE TOTALLY GULLIBLE?
DASH! VIOLET! I'M HURT! YOU THINK I'M LYING? WHAT'S NOT TO BELIEVE?

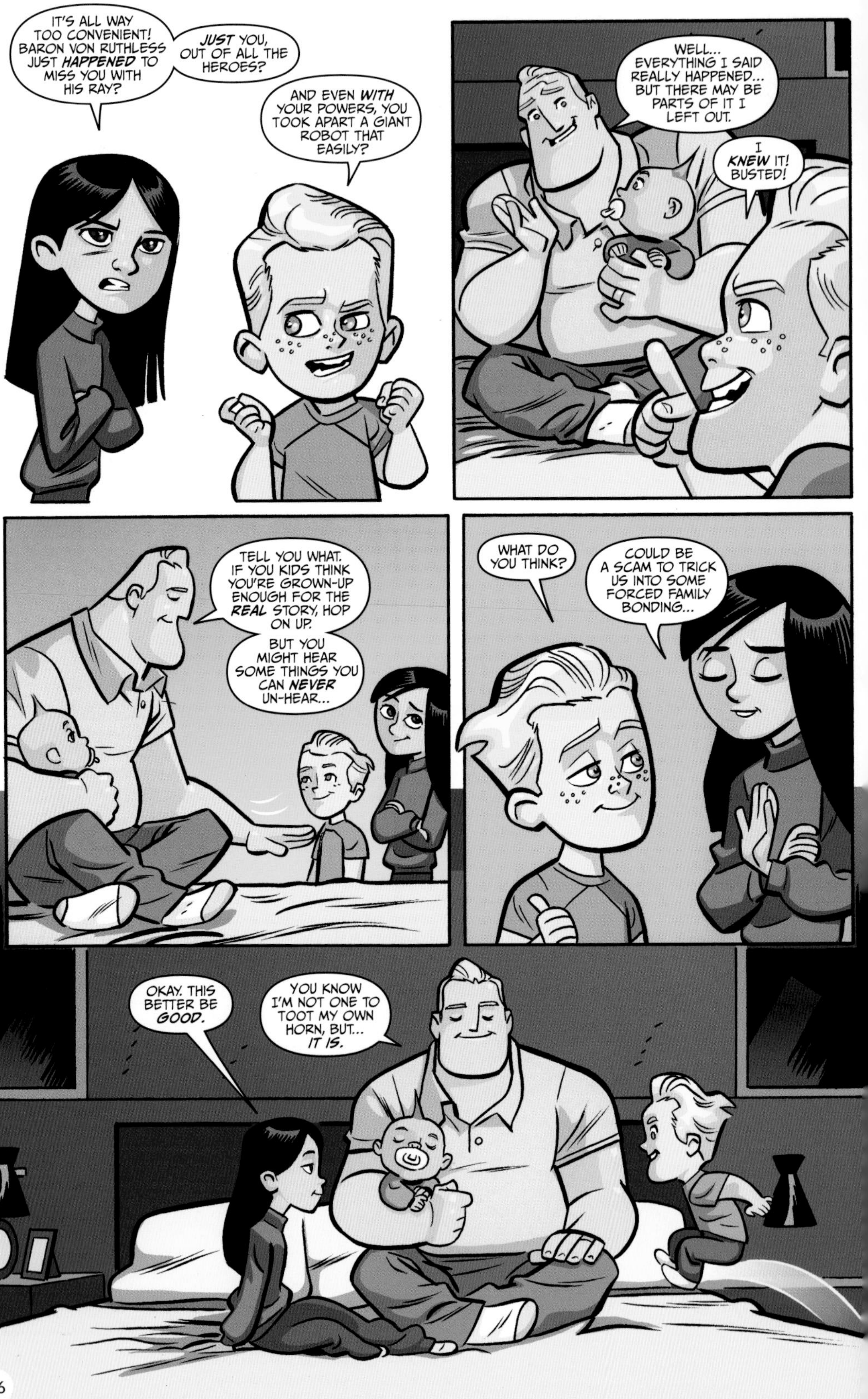
IT'S ALL WAY TOO CONVENIENT! BARON VON RUTHLESS JUST HAPPENED TO MISS YOU WITH HIS RAY?
JUST YOU, OUT OF ALL THE HEROES?
AND EVEN WITH YOUR POWERS, YOU TOOK APART A GIANT ROBOT THAT EASILY?
WELL... EVERYTHING I SAID REALLY HAPPENED... BUT THERE MAY BE PARTS OF IT I LEFT OUT.
I KNEW IT! BUSTED!
TELL YOU WHAT. IF YOU KIDS THINK YOU'RE GROWN-UP ENOUGH FOR THE REAL STORY, HOP ON UP.
BUT YOU MIGHT HEAR SOME THINGS YOU CAN NEVER UN-HEAR...
WHAT DO YOU THINK?
COULD BE A SCAM TO TRICK US INTO SOME FORCED FAMILY BONDING...
OKAY. THIS BETTER BE GOOD.
YOU KNOW I'M NOT ONE TO TOOT MY OWN HORN, BUT... IT IS.

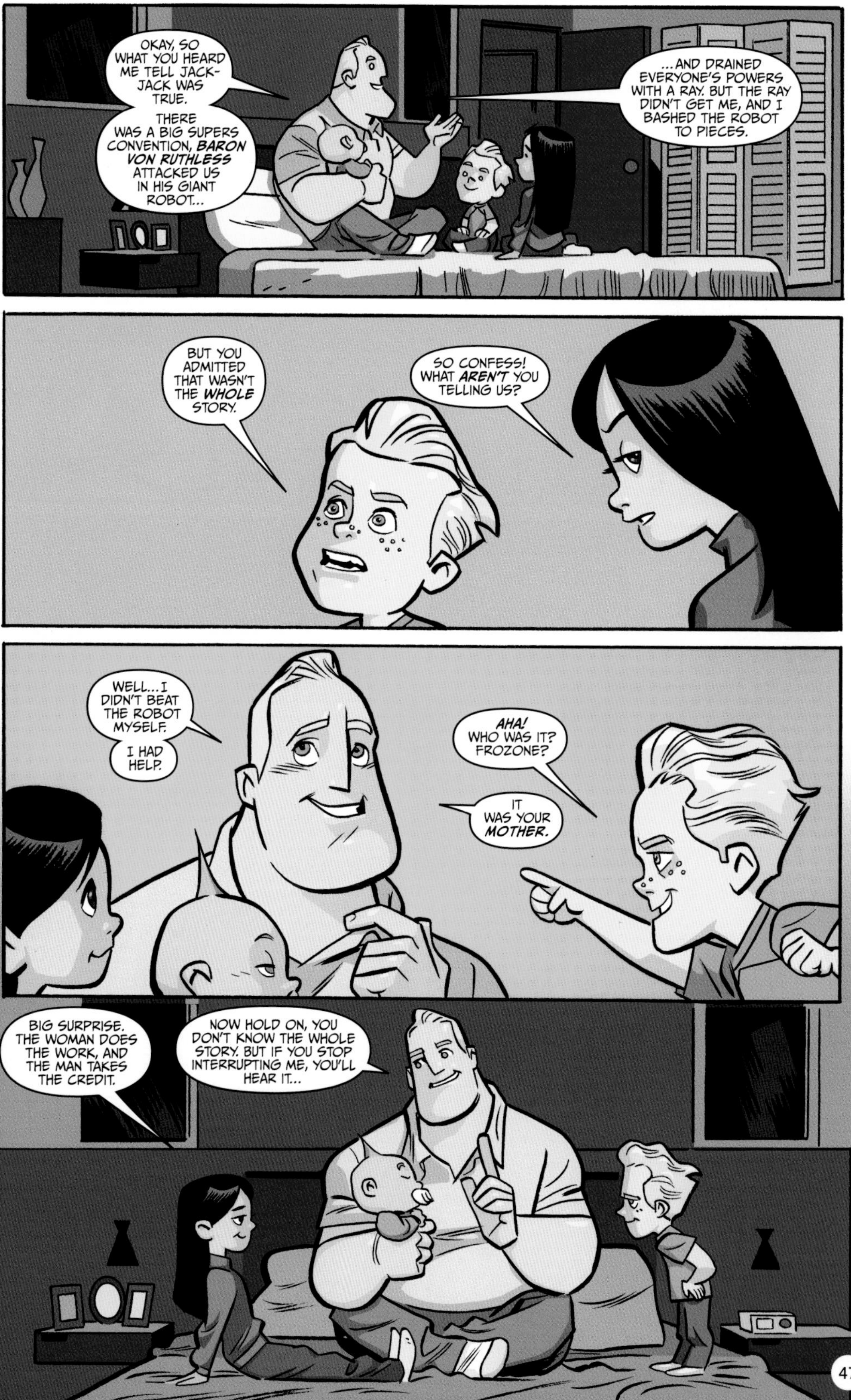
OKAY, SO WHAT YOU HEARD ME TELL JACK-JACK WAS TRUE.
THERE WAS A BIG SUPERS CONVENTION, BARON VON RUTHLESS ATTACKED US IN HIS GIANT ROBOT...
...AND DRAINED EVERYONE'S POWERS WITH A RAY. BUT THE RAY DIDN'T GET ME, AND I BASHED THE ROBOT TO PIECES.
BUT YOU ADMITTED THAT WASN'T THE WHOLE STORY.
SO CONFESS! WHAT AREN'T YOU TELLING US?
WELL...I DIDN'T BEAT THE ROBOT MYSELF.
I HAD HELP.
AHA! WHO WAS IT? FROZONE?
IT WAS YOUR MOTHER.
BIG SURPRISE. THE WOMAN DOES THE WORK, AND THE MAN TAKES THE CREDIT.
NOW HOLD ON, YOU DON'T KNOW THE WHOLE STORY. BUT IF YOU STOP INTERRUPTING ME, YOU'LL HEAR IT...

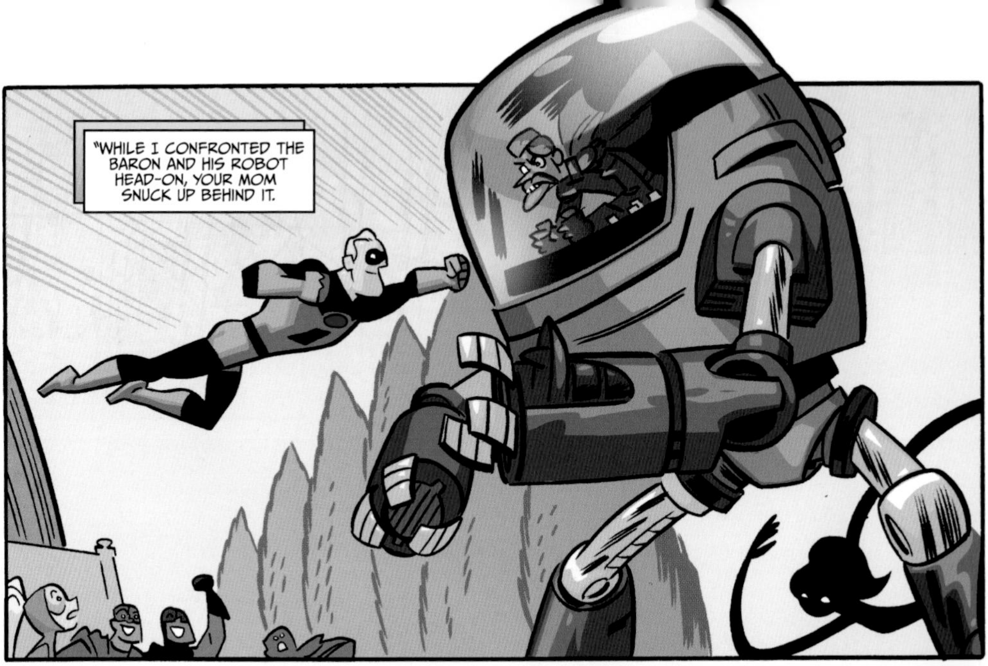
"WHILE I CONFRONTED THE BARON AND HIS ROBOT HEAD-ON, YOUR MOM SNUCK UP BEHIND IT.

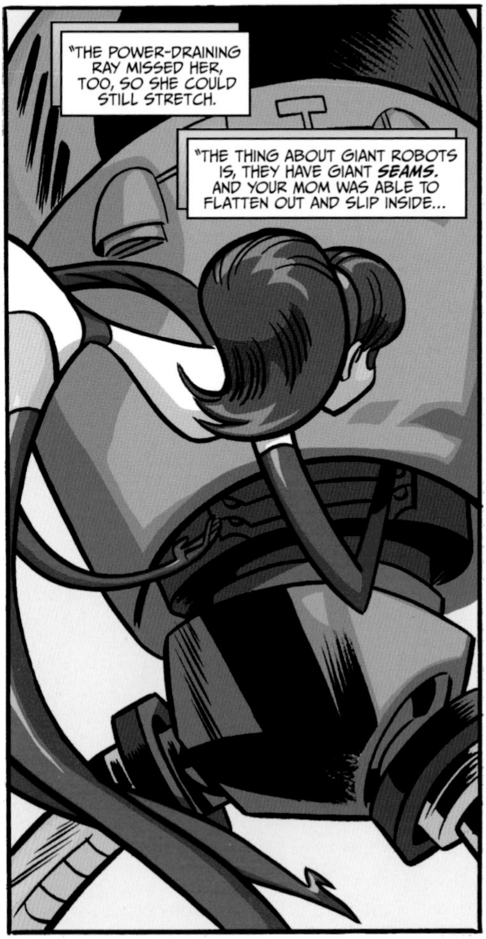
"THE POWER-DRAINING RAY MISSED HER, TOO, SO SHE COULD STILL STRETCH.
"THE THING ABOUT GIANT ROBOTS IS, THEY HAVE GIANT SEAMS. AND YOUR MOM WAS ABLE TO FLATTEN OUT AND SLIP INSIDE...

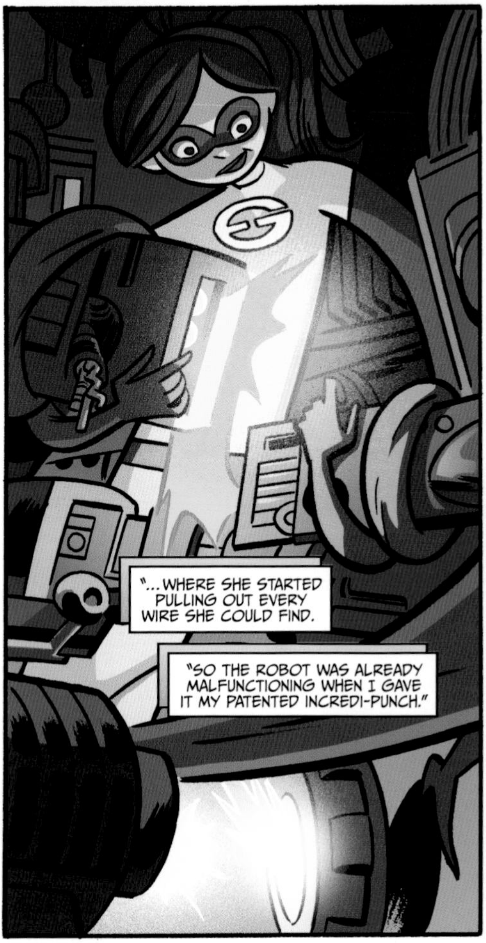
"...WHERE SHE STARTED PULLING OUT EVERY WIRE SHE COULD FIND.
"SO THE ROBOT WAS ALREADY MALFUNCTIONING WHEN I GAVE IT MY PATENTED INCREDI-PUNCH."

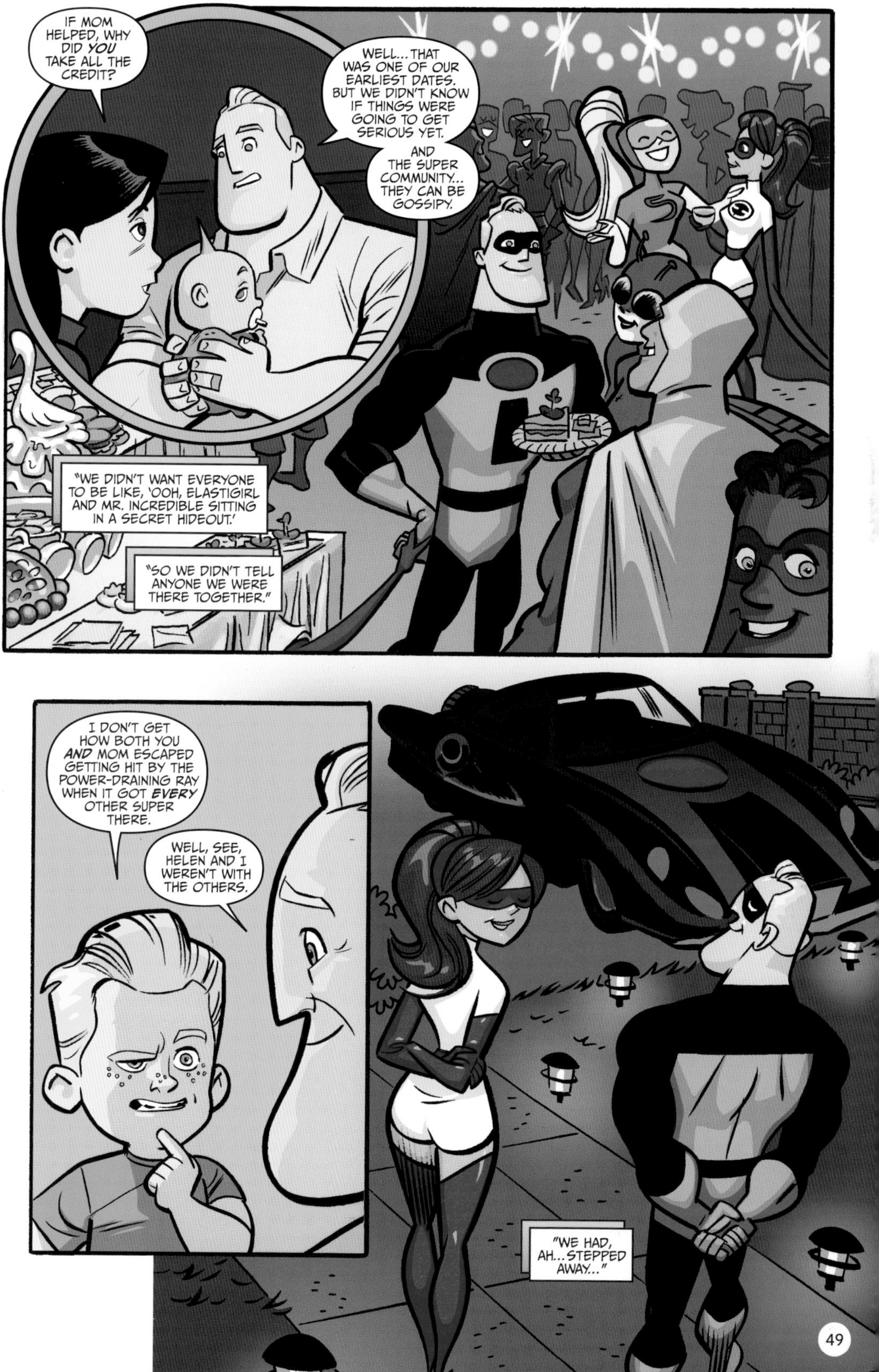

IF MOM HELPED, WHY DID YOU TAKE ALL THE CREDIT?
WELL... THAT WAS ONE OF OUR EARLIEST DATES. BUT WE DIDN'T KNOW IF THINGS WERE GOING TO GET SERIOUS YET.
AND THE SUPER COMMUNITY... THEY CAN BE GOSSIPY.
"WE DIDN'T WANT EVERYONE TO BE LIKE, 'OOH, ELASTIGIRL AND MR. INCREDIBLE SITTING IN A SECRET HIDEOUT.'
"SO WE DIDN'T TELL ANYONE WE WERE THERE TOGETHER."
I DON'T GET HOW BOTH YOU AND MOM ESCAPED GETTING HIT BY THE POWER-DRAINING RAY WHEN IT GOT EVERY OTHER SUPER THERE.
WELL, SEE, HELEN AND I WEREN'T WITH THE OTHERS.
"WE HAD, AH... STEPPED AWAY..."

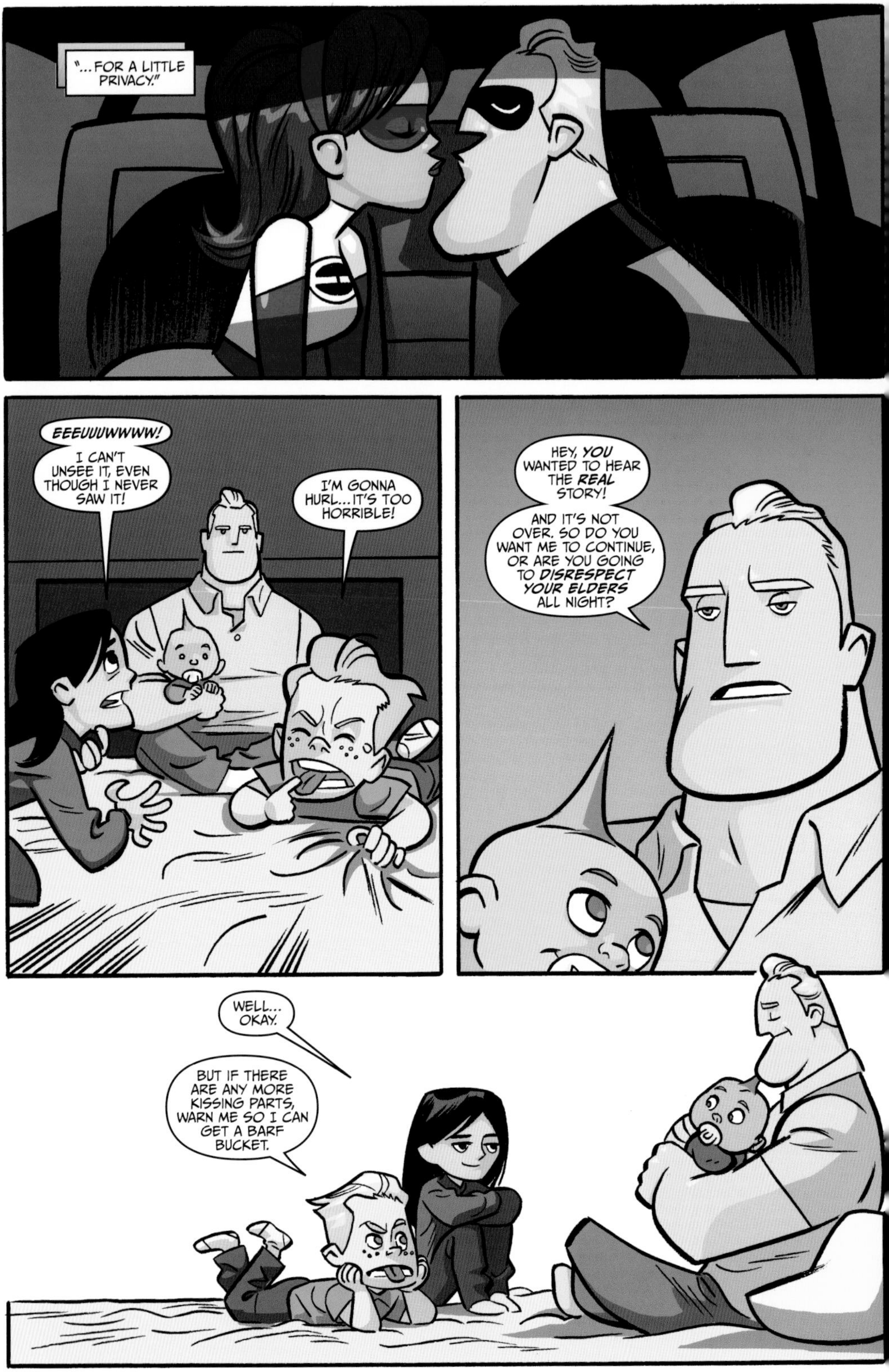
"...FOR A LITTLE PRIVACY."
EEEUUUWWWW!
I CAN'T UNSEE IT, EVEN THOUGH I NEVER SAW IT!
I'M GONNA HURL...IT'S TOO HORRIBLE!
HEY, YOU WANTED TO HEAR THE REAL STORY!
AND IT'S NOT OVER. SO DO YOU WANT ME TO CONTINUE, OR ARE YOU GOING TO DISRESPECT YOUR ELDERS ALL NIGHT?
WELL... OKAY.
BUT IF THERE ARE ANY MORE KISSING PARTS, WARN ME SO I CAN GET A BARF BUCKET.

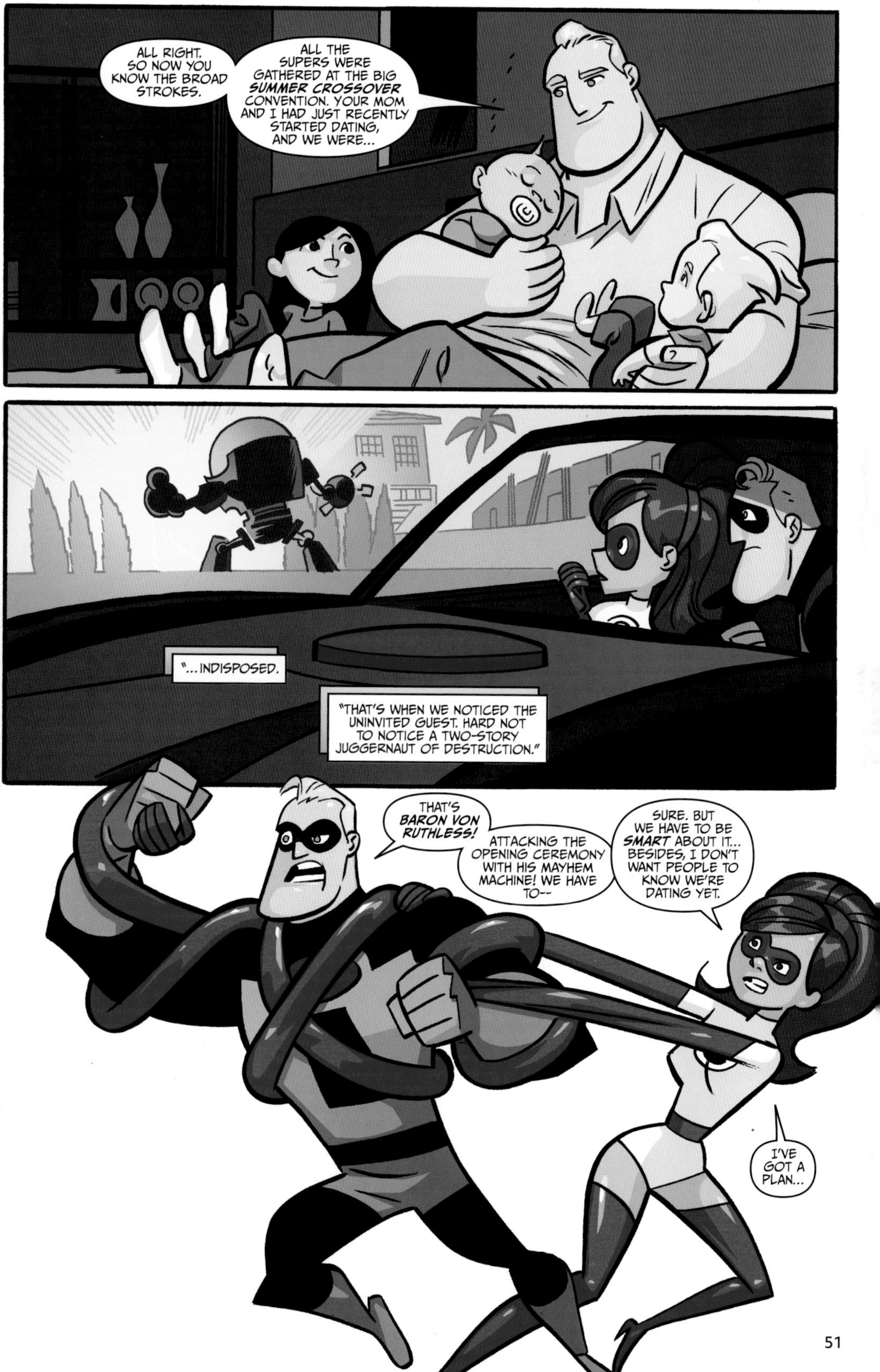
ALL RIGHT. SO NOW YOU KNOW THE BROAD STROKES.
ALL THE SUPERS WERE GATHERED AT THE BIG SUMMER CROSSOVER CONVENTION. YOUR MOM AND I HAD JUST RECENTLY STARTED DATING, AND WE WERE...
"...INDISPOSED.
"THAT'S WHEN WE NOTICED THE UNINVITED GUEST. HARD NOT TO NOTICE A TWO-STORY JUGGERNAUT OF DESTRUCTION."
THAT'S BARON VON RUTHLESS!
ATTACKING THE OPENING CEREMONY WITH HIS MAYHEM MACHINE! WE HAVE TO--
SURE. BUT WE HAVE TO BE SMART ABOUT IT... BESIDES, I DON'T WANT PEOPLE TO KNOW WE'RE DATING YET.
I'VE GOT A PLAN...

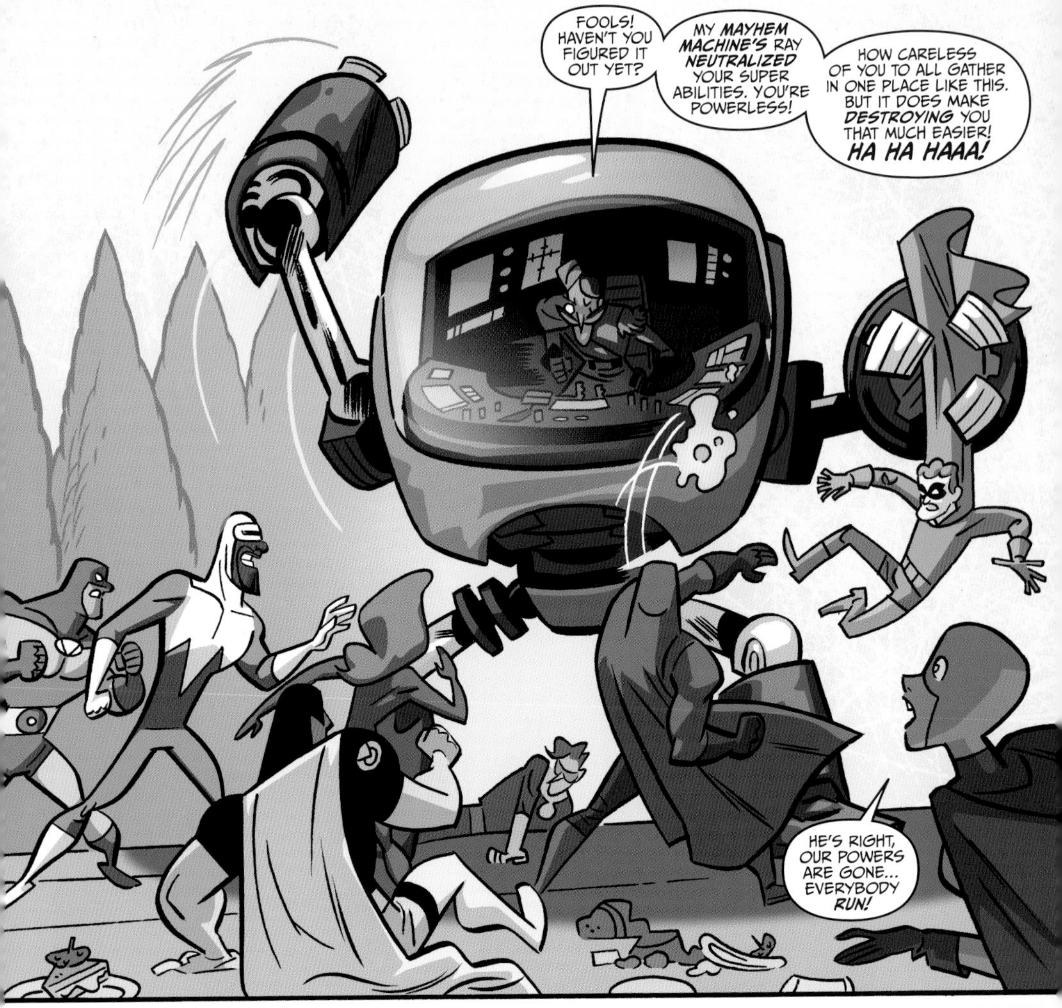
FOOLS! HAVEN'T YOU FIGURED IT OUT YET?
MY MAYHEM MACHINE'S RAY NEUTRALIZED YOUR SUPER ABILITIES. YOU'RE POWERLESS!
HOW CARELESS OF YOU TO ALL GATHER IN ONE PLACE LIKE THIS. BUT IT DOES MAKE DESTROYING YOU THAT MUCH EASIER! HA HA HAAA!
HE'S RIGHT, OUR POWERS ARE GONE... EVERYBODY RUN!

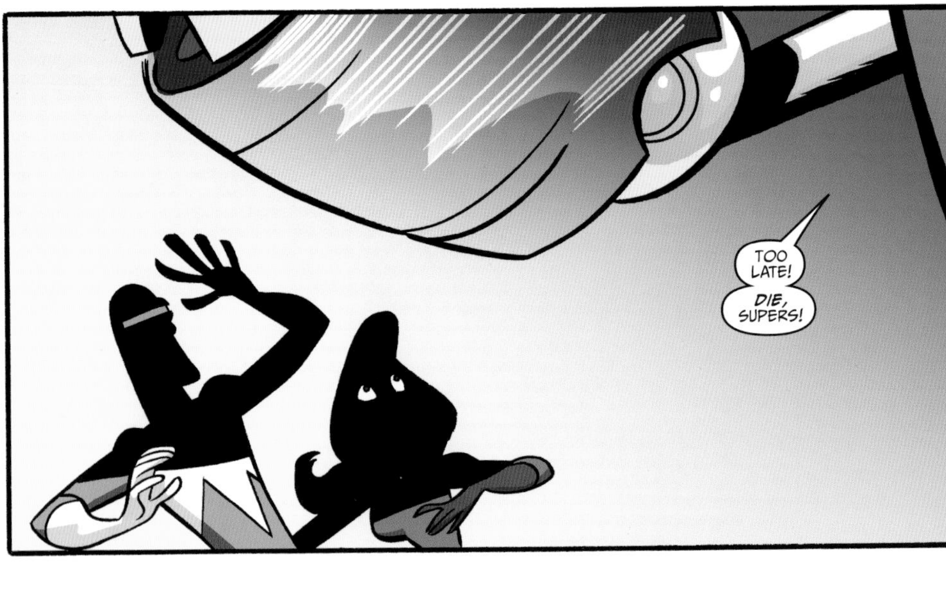
TOO LATE!
DIE, SUPERS!

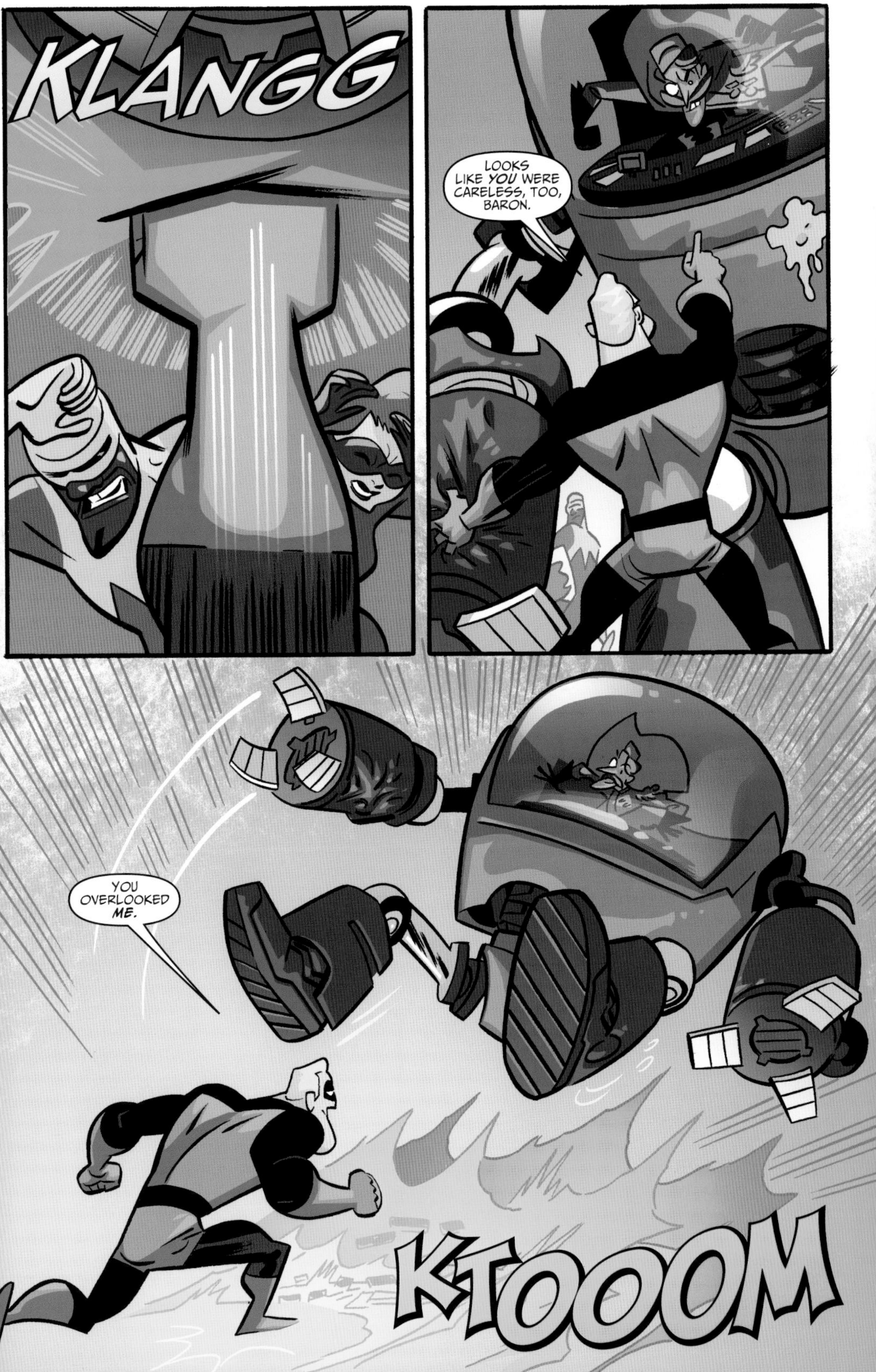
KLANGG
LOOKS LIKE YOU WERE CARELESS, TOO, BARON.
YOU OVERLOOKED ME.
KTOOOM

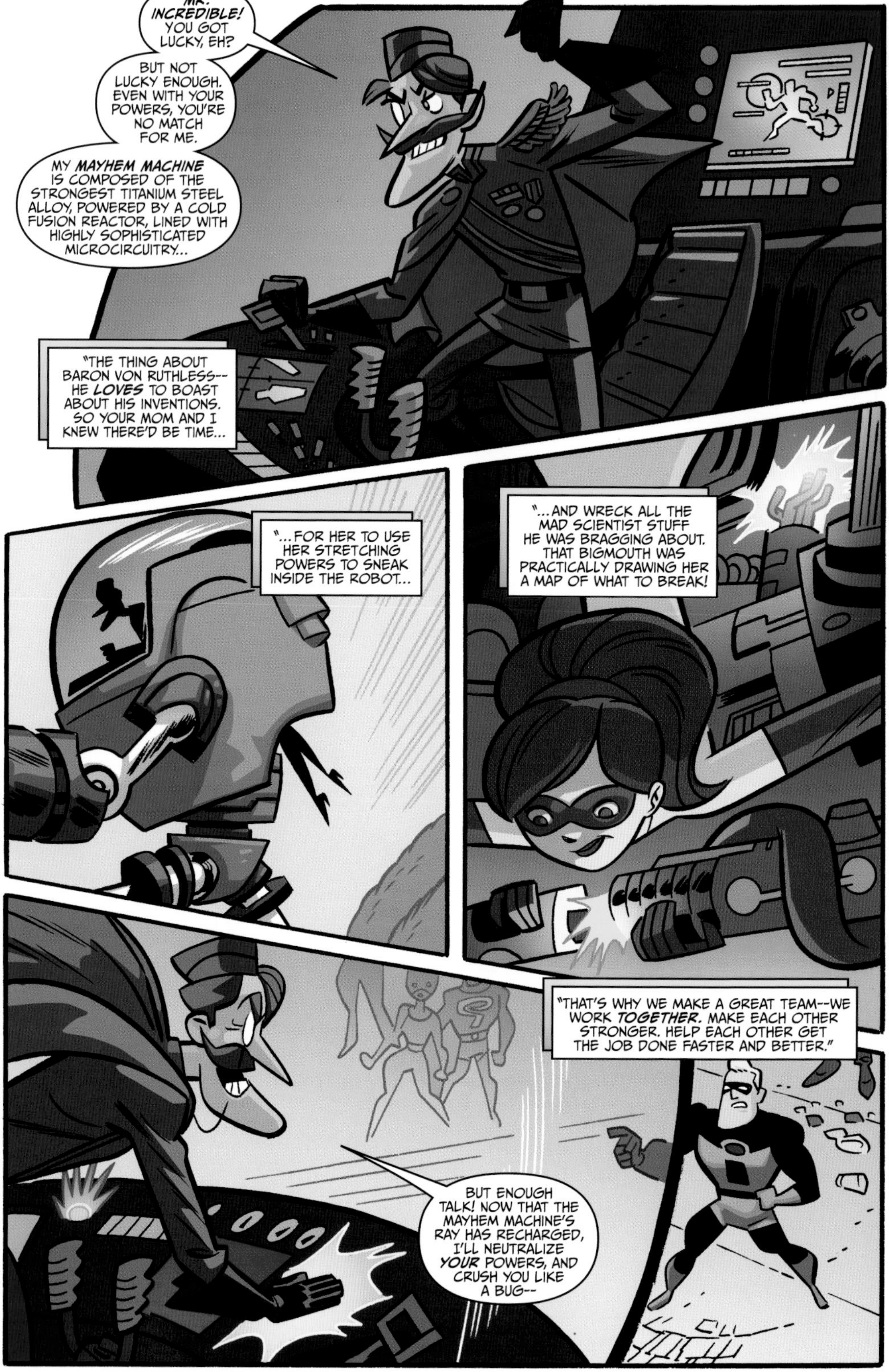
MR. INCREDIBLE! YOU GOT LUCKY, EH?
BUT NOT LUCKY ENOUGH. EVEN WITH YOUR POWERS, YOU'RE NO MATCH FOR ME.
MY MAYHEM MACHINE IS COMPOSED OF THE STRONGEST TITANIUM STEEL ALLOY, POWERED BY A COLD FUSION REACTOR, LINED WITH HIGHLY SOPHISTICATED MICROCIRCUITRY...
"THE THING ABOUT BARON VON RUTHLESS-- HE LOVES TO BOAST ABOUT HIS INVENTIONS. SO YOUR MOM AND I KNEW THERE'D BE TIME...
"...FOR HER TO USE HER STRETCHING POWERS TO SNEAK INSIDE THE ROBOT...
"...AND WRECK ALL THE MAD SCIENTIST STUFF HE WAS BRAGGING ABOUT. THAT BIGMOUTH WAS PRACTICALLY DRAWING HER A MAP OF WHAT TO BREAK!
"THAT'S WHY WE MAKE A GREAT TEAM--WE WORK TOGETHER. MAKE EACH OTHER STRONGER. HELP EACH OTHER GET THE JOB DONE FASTER AND BETTER."
BUT ENOUGH TALK! NOW THAT THE MAYHEM MACHINE'S RAY HAS RECHARGED, I'LL NEUTRALIZE YOUR POWERS, AND CRUSH YOU LIKE A BUG--

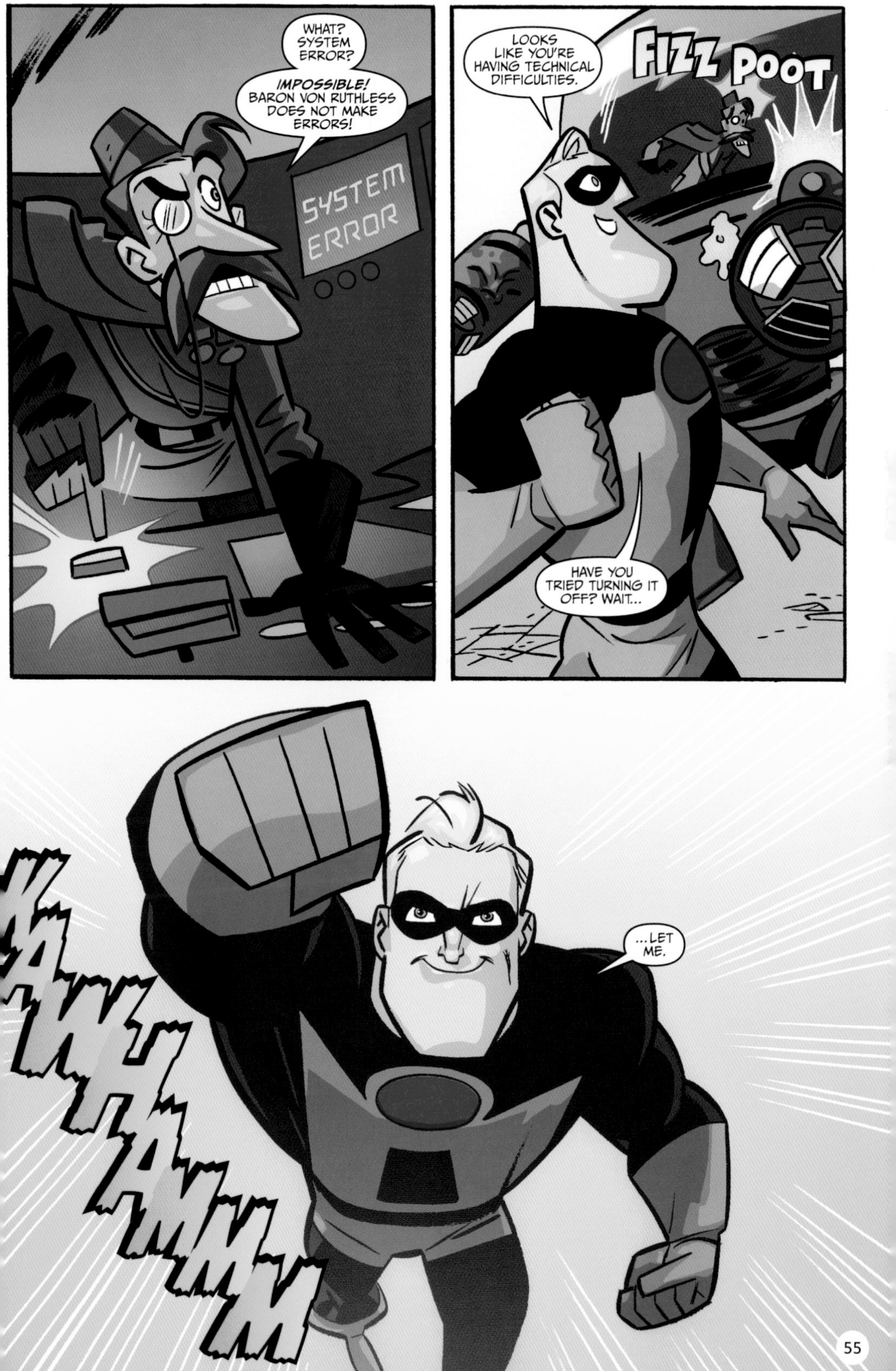
WHAT? SYSTEM ERROR?
IMPOSSIBLE! BARON VON RUTHLESS DOES NOT MAKE ERRORS!
SYSTEM ERROR
LOOKS LIKE YOU'RE HAVING TECHNICAL DIFFICULTIES.
FIZZ POOT
HAVE YOU TRIED TURNING IT OFF? WAIT...
KAWHAMMM
...LET ME.

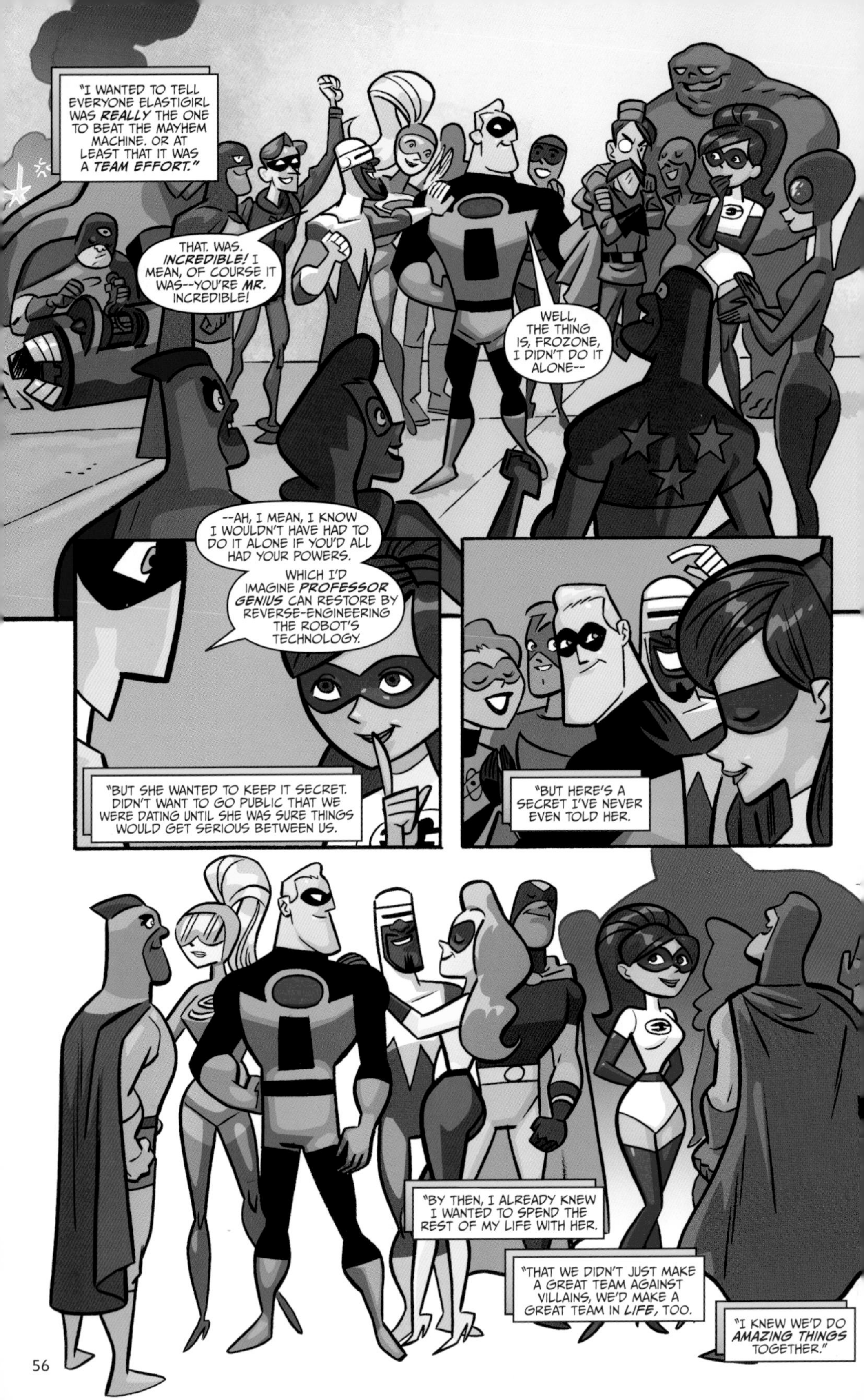
"I WANTED TO TELL EVERYONE ELASTIGIRL WAS ***REALLY*** THE ONE TO BEAT THE MAYHEM MACHINE. OR AT LEAST THAT IT WAS A ***TEAM EFFORT.***"
THAT. WAS. ***INCREDIBLE!*** I MEAN, OF COURSE IT WAS--YOU'RE ***MR.*** INCREDIBLE!
WELL, THE THING IS, FROZONE, I DIDN'T DO IT ALONE--
--AH, I MEAN, I KNOW I WOULDN'T HAVE HAD TO DO IT ALONE IF YOU'D ALL HAD YOUR POWERS.
WHICH I'D IMAGINE ***PROFESSOR GENIUS*** CAN RESTORE BY REVERSE-ENGINEERING THE ROBOT'S TECHNOLOGY.
"BUT SHE WANTED TO KEEP IT SECRET. DIDN'T WANT TO GO PUBLIC THAT WE WERE DATING UNTIL SHE WAS SURE THINGS WOULD GET SERIOUS BETWEEN US.
"BUT HERE'S A SECRET I'VE NEVER EVEN TOLD HER.
"BY THEN, I ALREADY KNEW I WANTED TO SPEND THE REST OF MY LIFE WITH HER.
"THAT WE DIDN'T JUST MAKE A GREAT TEAM AGAINST VILLAINS, WE'D MAKE A GREAT TEAM IN ***LIFE,*** TOO.
"I KNEW WE'D DO ***AMAZING THINGS*** TOGETHER."

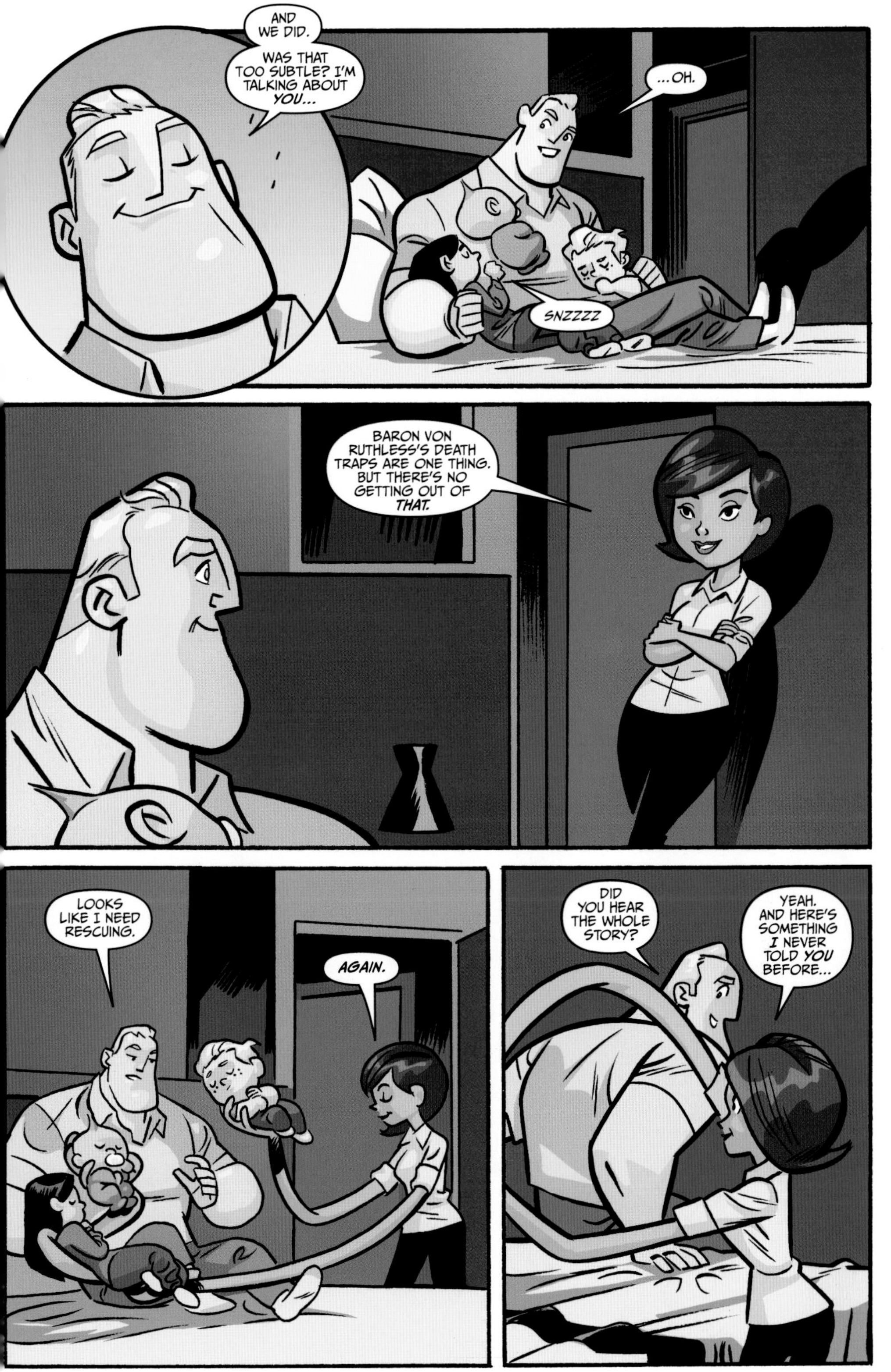

AND WE DID.
WAS THAT TOO SUBTLE? I'M TALKING ABOUT YOU...
...OH.
SNZZZZ
BARON VON RUTHLESS'S DEATH TRAPS ARE ONE THING. BUT THERE'S NO GETTING OUT OF THAT.
LOOKS LIKE I NEED RESCUING.
AGAIN.
DID YOU HEAR THE WHOLE STORY?
YEAH. AND HERE'S SOMETHING I NEVER TOLD YOU BEFORE...

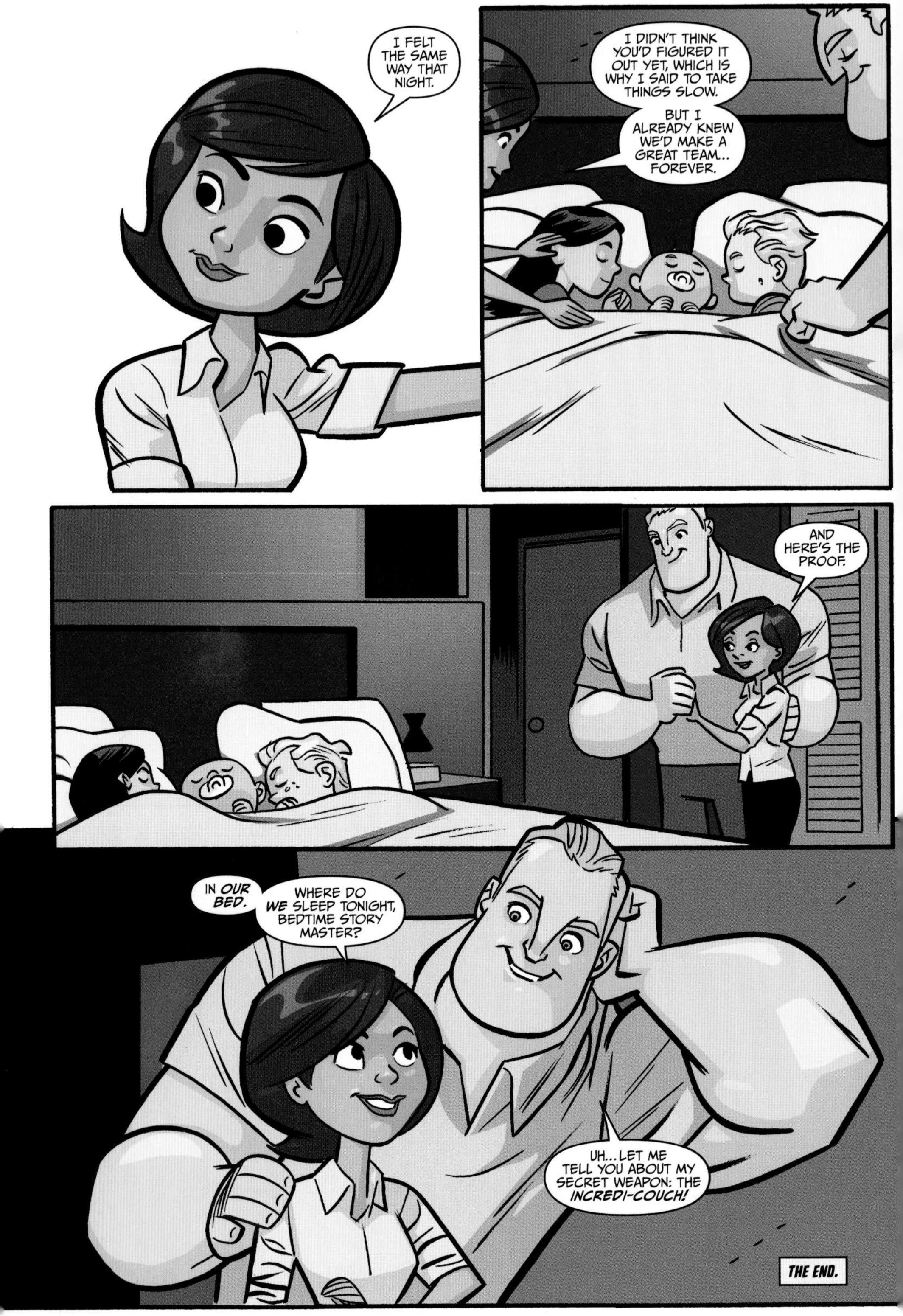
I FELT THE SAME WAY THAT NIGHT.
I DIDN'T THINK YOU'D FIGURED IT OUT YET, WHICH IS WHY I SAID TO TAKE THINGS SLOW.
BUT I ALREADY KNEW WE'D MAKE A GREAT TEAM... FOREVER.
AND HERE'S THE PROOF.
WHERE DO *WE* SLEEP TONIGHT, BEDTIME STORY MASTER?
IN *OUR BED.*
UH...LET ME TELL YOU ABOUT MY SECRET WEAPON: THE *INCREDI-COUCH!*
THE END.

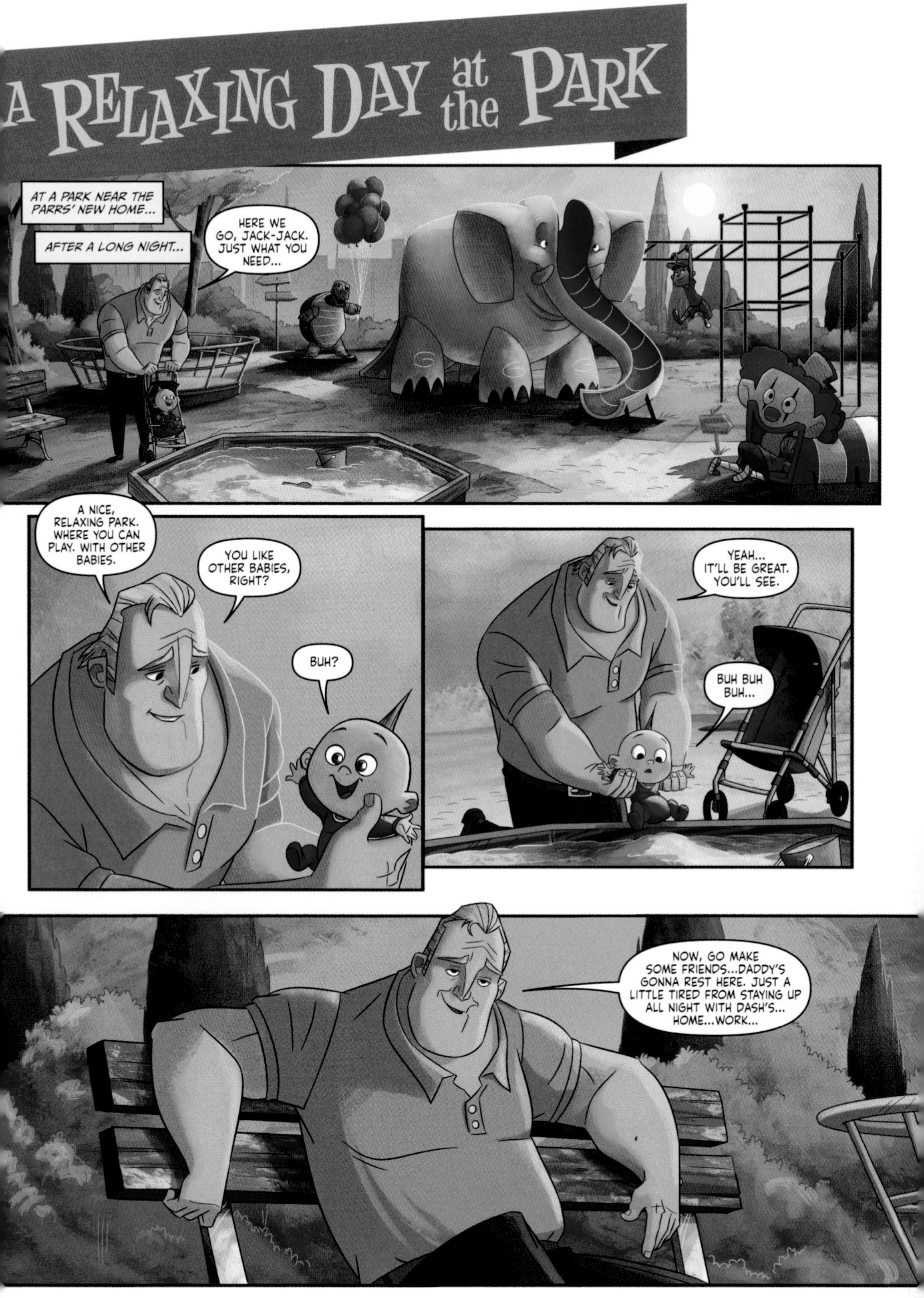
A RELAXING DAY at the PARK
AT A PARK NEAR THE PARRS' NEW HOME...
AFTER A LONG NIGHT...
HERE WE GO, JACK-JACK. JUST WHAT YOU NEED...
A NICE, RELAXING PARK. WHERE YOU CAN PLAY. WITH OTHER BABIES.
YOU LIKE OTHER BABIES, RIGHT?
BUH?
YEAH... IT'LL BE GREAT. YOU'LL SEE.
BUH BUH BUH...
NOW, GO MAKE SOME FRIENDS...DADDY'S GONNA REST HERE. JUST A LITTLE TIRED FROM STAYING UP ALL NIGHT WITH DASH'S... HOME...WORK...

ZZZZZZZ

AGUH BAH!

WWWAAAAAAHHHH!

GUH WUH!

Howdy do, kids!

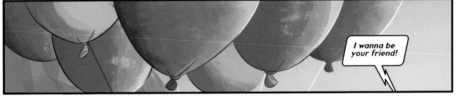

I wanna be your friend!

WWAAAAAAHH

GAH BUH!

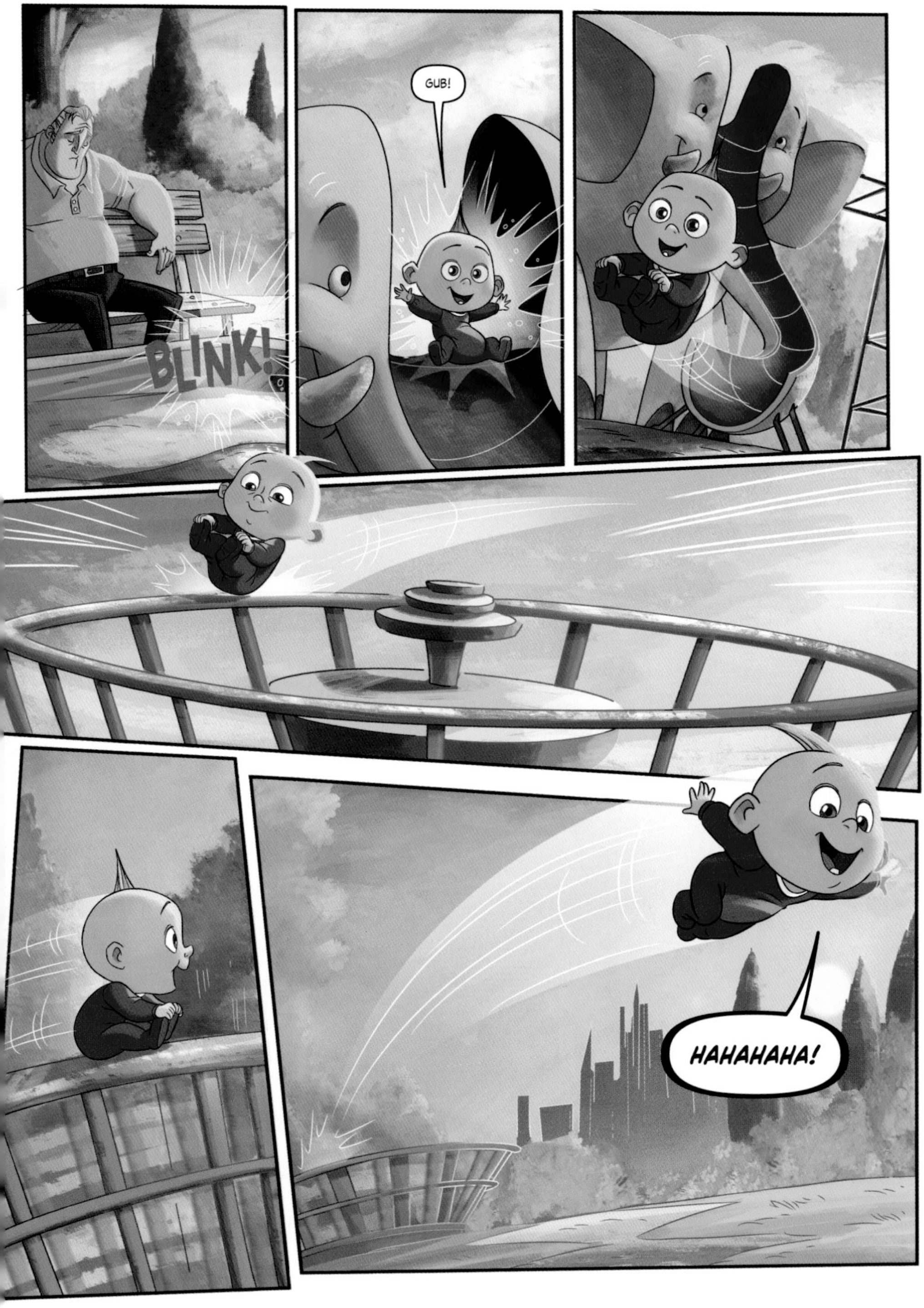
BLINK!
GUB!
HAHAHAHA!

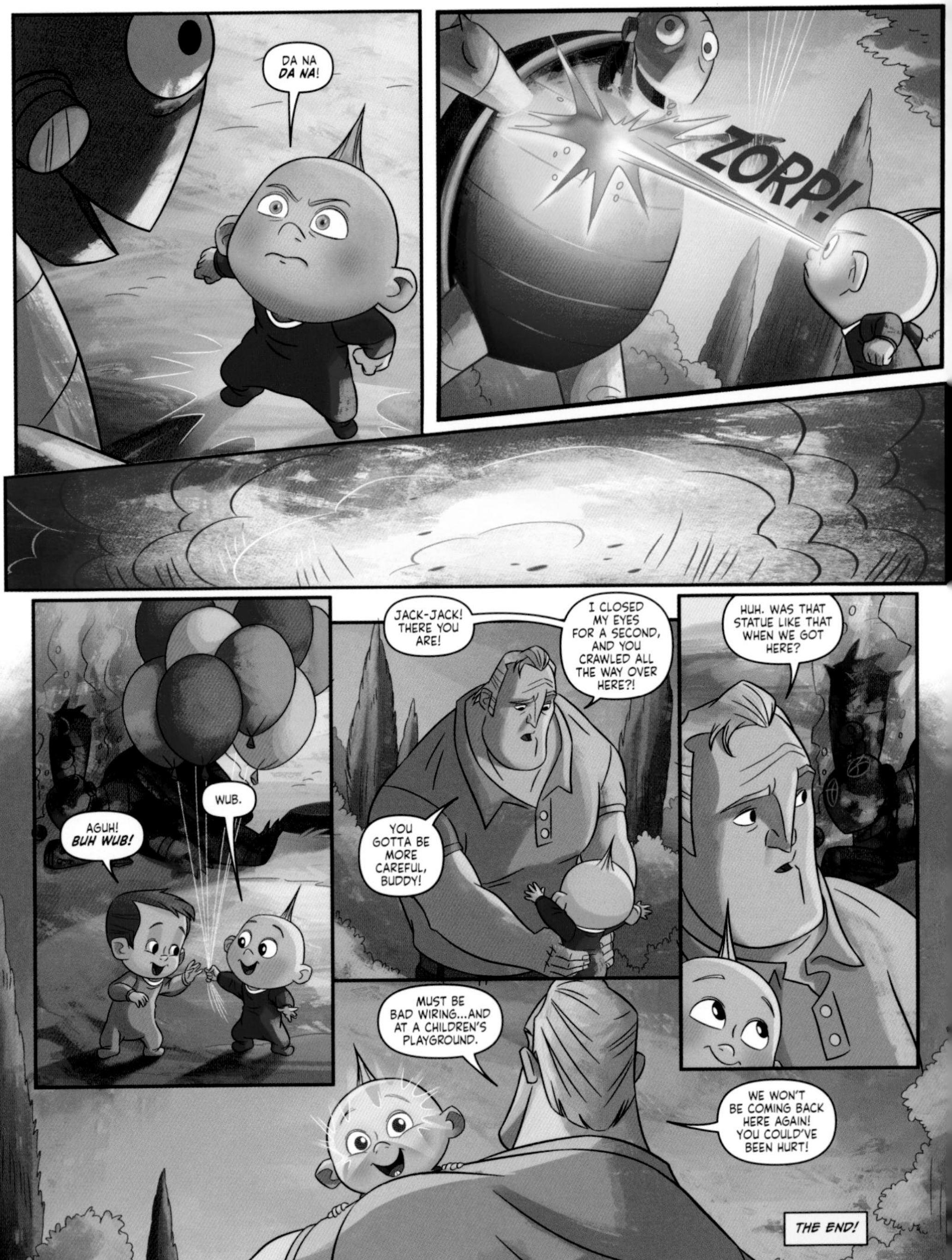

DA NA DA NA!
ZORP!
AGUH! BUH WUB!
WUB.
JACK-JACK! THERE YOU ARE!
I CLOSED MY EYES FOR A SECOND, AND YOU CRAWLED ALL THE WAY OVER HERE?!
YOU GOTTA BE MORE CAREFUL, BUDDY!
HUH. WAS THAT STATUE LIKE THAT WHEN WE GOT HERE?
MUST BE BAD WIRING...AND AT A CHILDREN'S PLAYGROUND.
WE WON'T BE COMING BACK HERE AGAIN! YOU COULD'VE BEEN HURT!
THE END!

HOW the COOKIE CRUMBLES

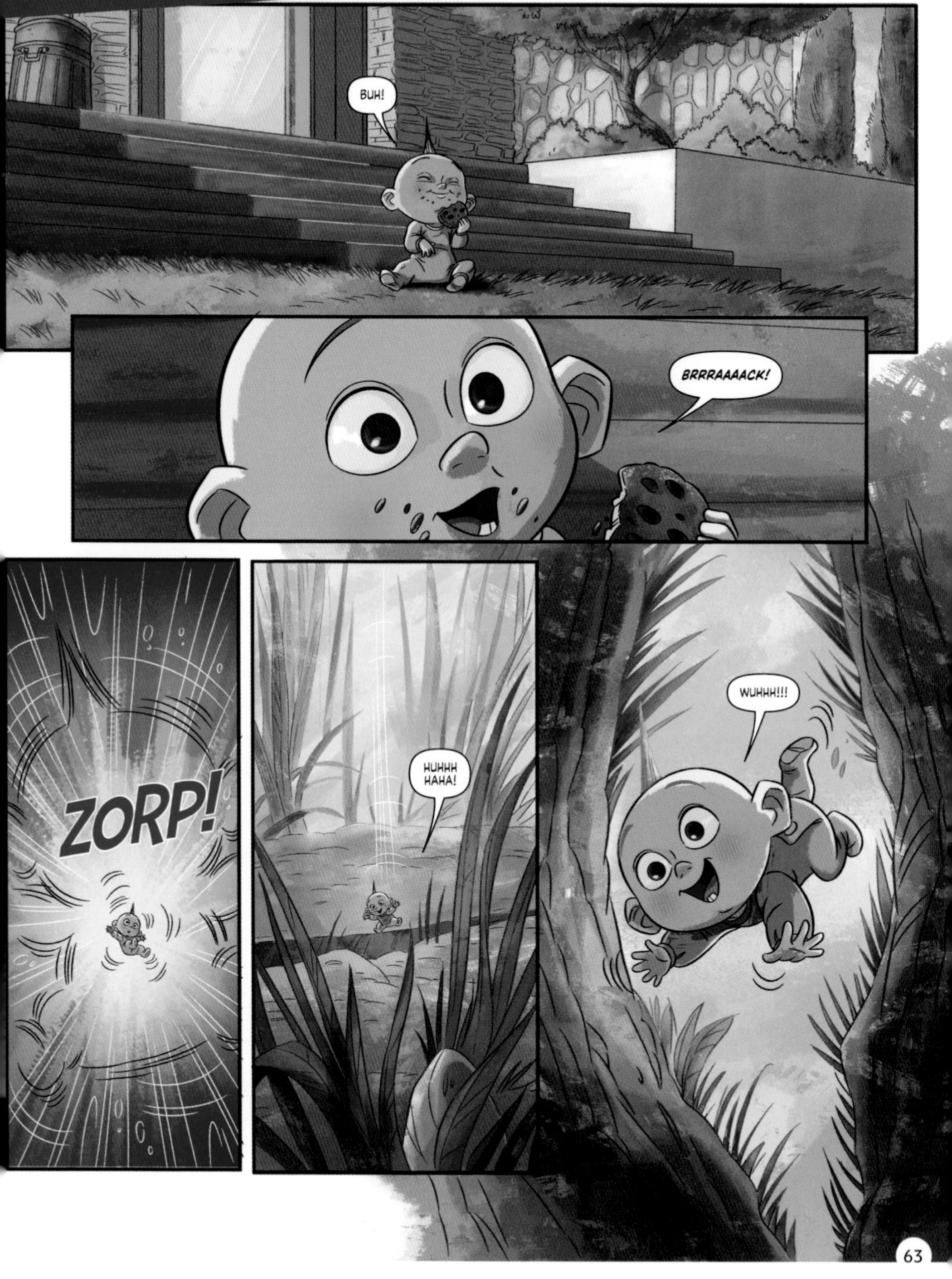
BUH!
BRRRAAAACK!
ZORP!
HUHHH HAHA!
WUHHH!!!

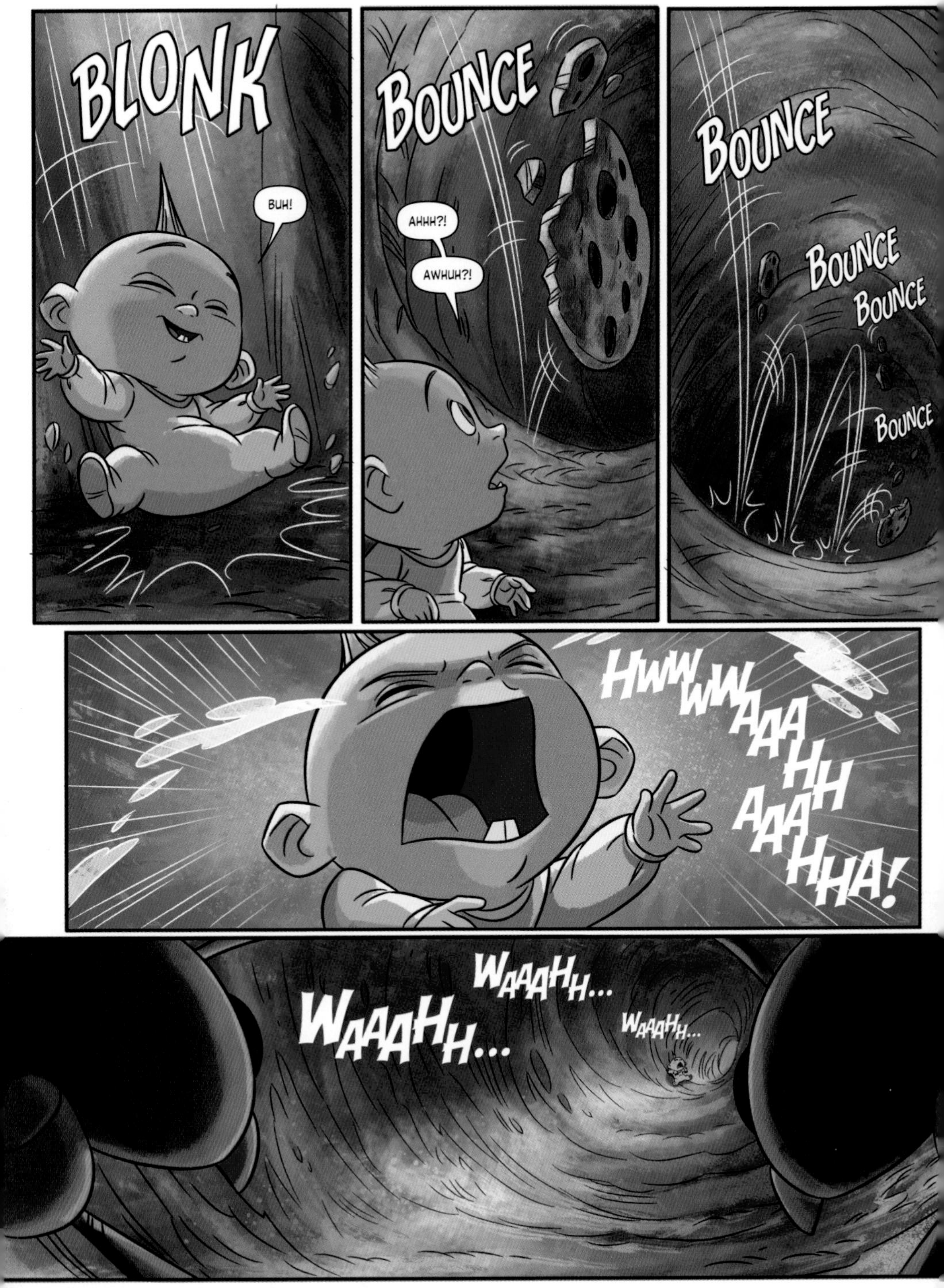
BLONK
BUH!
BOUNCE
AHHH?!
AWHUH?!
BOUNCE
BOUNCE
BOUNCE
BOUNCE
HWWWWAAAHHAAAHHA!
WAAAHH...
WAAAHH...
WAAAHH...

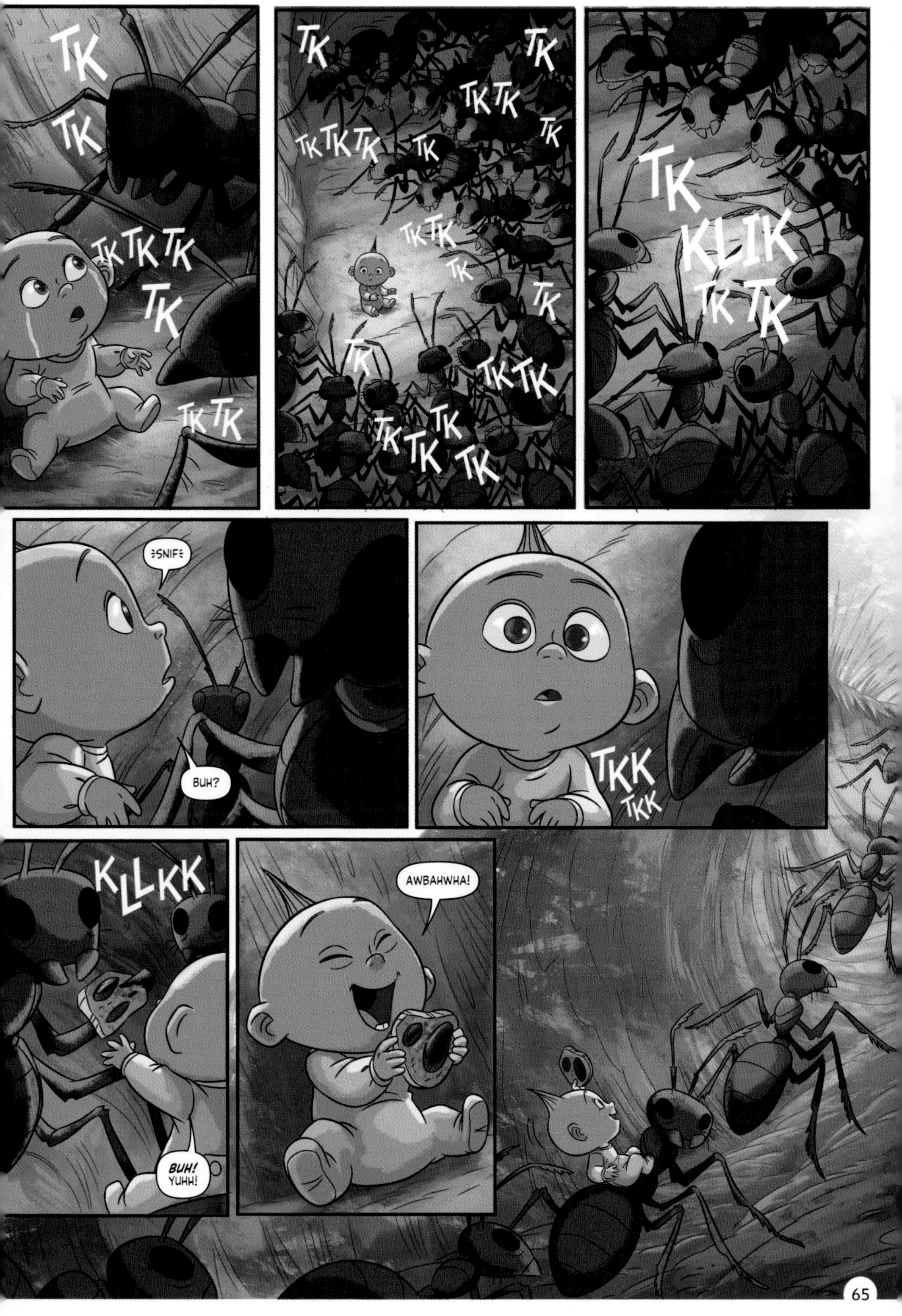
TK
TK
TK TK TK
TK
TK TK
TK
TK
TK TK
TK
TK TK TK
TK
TK TK
TK
TK
TK
TK TK
TK TK
TK
TK
TK
TK
KLIK
TK TK
SNIF
BUH?
TKK
TKK
KLLKK
BUH!
YUHH!
AWBAHWHA!

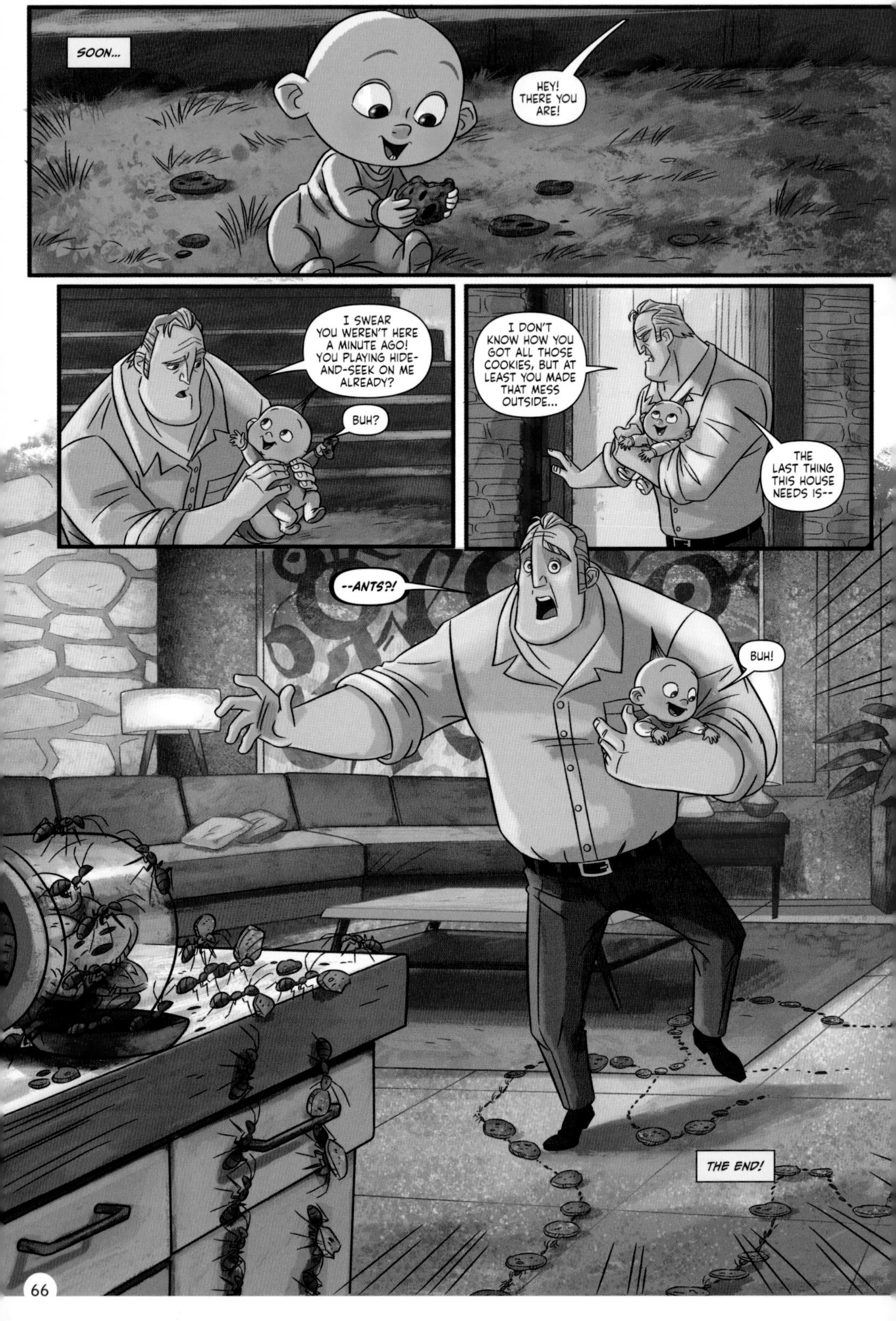
SOON...
HEY! THERE YOU ARE!
I SWEAR YOU WEREN'T HERE A MINUTE AGO! YOU PLAYING HIDE-AND-SEEK ON ME ALREADY?
BUH?
I DON'T KNOW HOW YOU GOT ALL THOSE COOKIES, BUT AT LEAST YOU MADE THAT MESS OUTSIDE...
THE LAST THING THIS HOUSE NEEDS IS--
--ANTS?!
BUH!
THE END!

Disney · PIXAR
INCREDIBLES 2

PIN-UP GALLERY

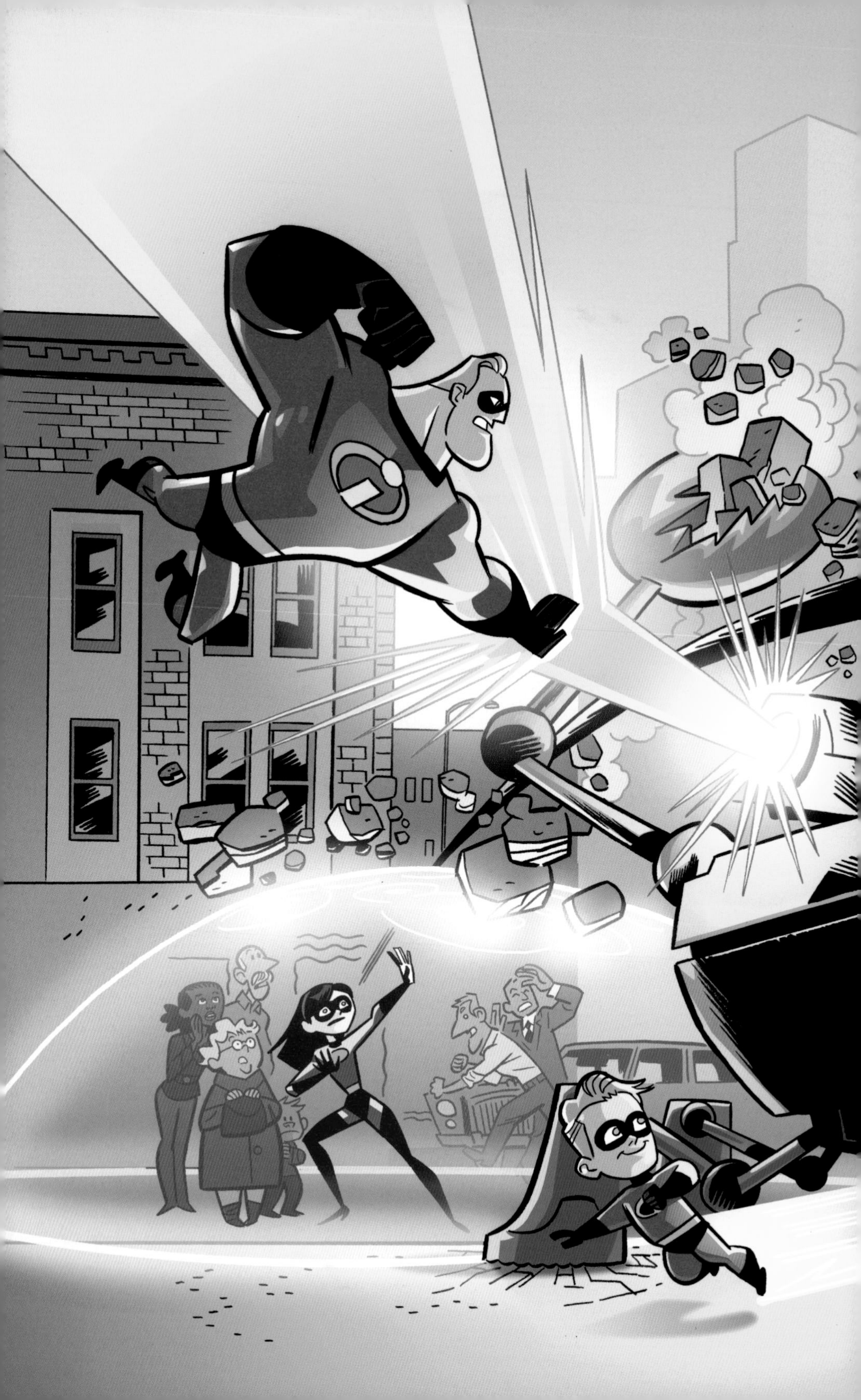

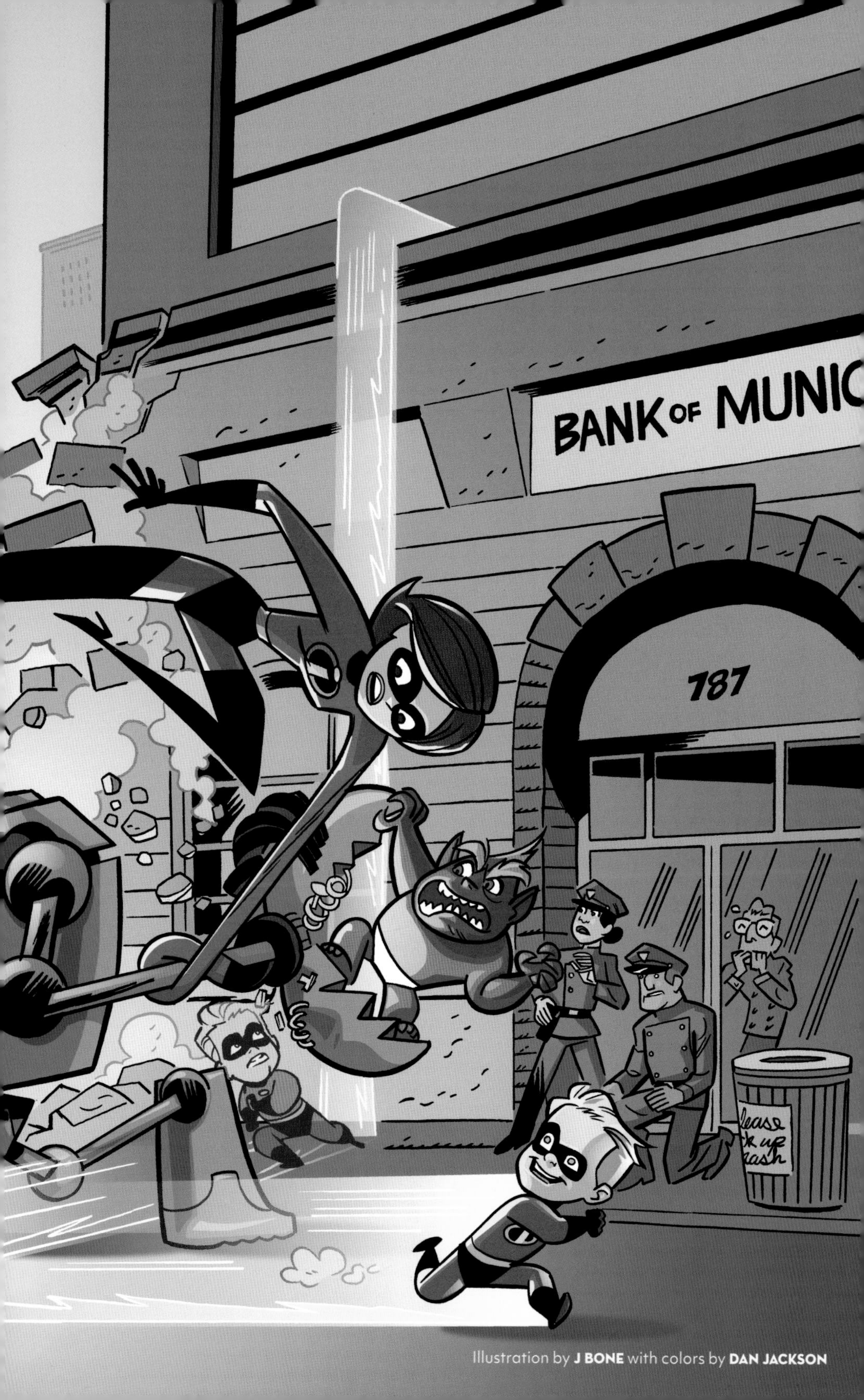
BANK OF MUNIC
787
Illustration by **J BONE** with colors by **DAN JACKSON**

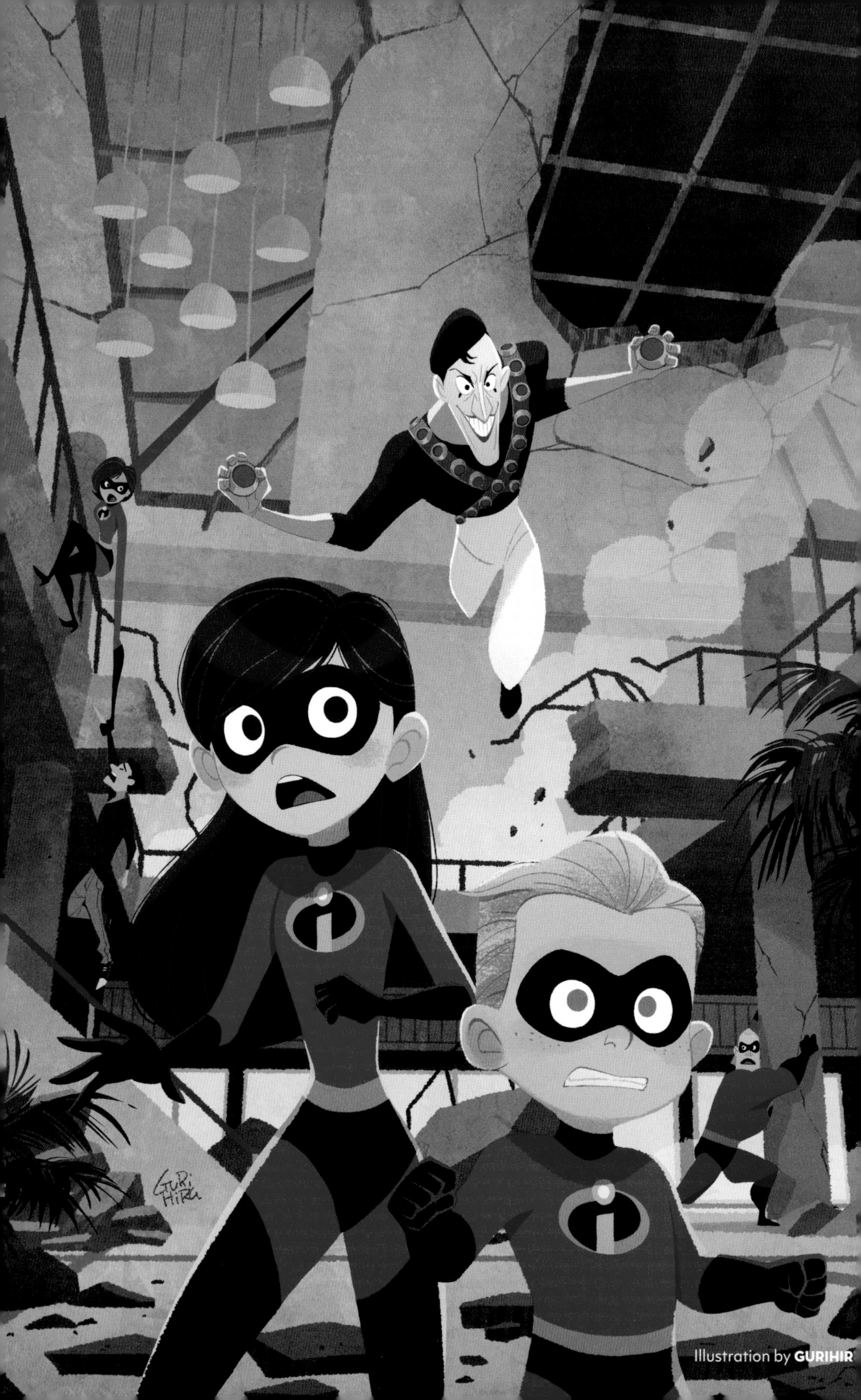

Illustration by **GURIHIR**

Disney · PIXAR
INCREDIBLES 2
Heroes at Home
Disney
COMICS

A Graphic Novel for Younger Readers
Disney
ZOOTOPIA
FRIENDS TO THE RESCUE
BUNNYBURROW
COUNTY FAIR
Disney
COMICS

A Graphic Novel for Younger Readers
Disney
PRINCESS
Jasmine's New Pet
Disney
COMICS

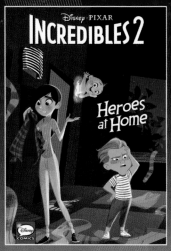

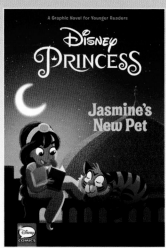

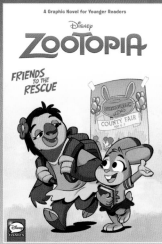

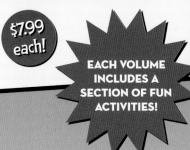

LOOKING FOR BOOKS FOR YOUNGER READERS?

$7.99 each!

EACH VOLUME INCLUDES A SECTION OF FUN ACTIVITIES!

DISNEY·PIXAR INCREDIBLES 2: HEROES AT HOME

Violet and Dash are part of a Super family, and they are trying to help out at home. Can they pick up groceries and secretly stop some bad guys? And then can they clean up the house while Jack-Jack is "sleeping"?

ISBN 978-1-50670-943-7 | $7.99

DISNEY ZOOTOPIA: FRIENDS TO THE RESCUE

Young Judy Hopps proves she's a brave little bunny when she helps a classmate. And can a quick-thinking young Nick Wilde liven up a birthday party? Friends save the day in these tales of Zootopia!

ISBN 978-1-50671-054-9 | $7.99

DISNEY PRINCESS: JASMINE'S NEW PET

Jasmine has a new pet tiger, Rajah, but he's not quite ready for palace life. Will she be able to train the young cub before the Sultan finds him another home?

ISBN 978-1-50671-052-5 | $7.99

AVAILABLE AT YOUR LOCAL COMICS SHOP OR BOOKSTORE! TO FIND A COMICS SHOP IN YOUR AREA, VISIT COMICSHOPLOCATOR.COM

DARK HORSE BOOKS

For more information or to order direct: On the web: DarkHorse.com | Email: mailorder@darkhorse.com
Phone: 1-800-862-0052 Mon.–Fri. 9 AM to 5 PM Pacific Time

Disney COMICS

CLASSIC STORIES RETOLD
WITH THE MAGIC OF DISNEY!

Disney Treasure Island, starring Mickey Mouse

Robert Louis Stevenson's classic tale of pirates, treasure, and swashbuckling adventure comes to life in this adaptation that stars Mickey, Goofy, and Pegleg Pete! When Jim Mousekins discovers a map to buried treasure, his dream of adventure is realized with a voyage on the high seas, a quest through tropical island jungles . . . and a race to evade cutthroat pirates!

978-1-50671-158-4 �֍ $10.99

Disney Moby Dick, starring Donald Duck

In an adaptation of Herman Melville's classic, Scrooge McDuck, Donald, and nephews venture out on the high seas in pursuit of the white whale Moby Dick who stole Captain Quackhab's lucky dime. As Quackhab scours the ocean in pursuit of his nemesis, facing other dangers of the sea, the crew begin to wonder: how far will their captain go for revenge?

978-1-50671-157-7 ✖ $10.99